CANDLELIGHT
AN EMBER SERIES NOVELLA

STACY McWILLIAMS

I'd like to dedicate this book to my aunt, Mary. She taught us all to take life as it comes and to appreciate the little moments, because all too soon those moments are all we have left. She was gone too soon from our lives, but will never be forgotten.

The ones we love never truly leave us; they walk beside us everyday unseen, unheard but always present, guiding, and loving us.

CHAPTER 1
NOT DEMON ENOUGH

Six in the morning was an unusual time for me to wake up, but as I took in the alarm clock blinking to my left, I realised that I'd awakened again for the third morning in a row at this time. I groaned and ran my fingers over my face as I tried to recall my dream. I remembered the feeling of horror all too well and the panic, but nothing else. Shaking my head, I dragged myself out of bed and walked over to my bathroom.

Barely glancing at myself in the mirror, I went about my business and decided that instead of trying to get back to sleep, I would go for a jog. I needed to clear my head and I didn't have an exam today; otherwise, I would probably use this time to study. As I walked over to my wardrobe, I searched for my running gear. It had been a few weeks since I'd been inclined to run, so I couldn't remember where I had left them.

My clothes were easy enough to find, but my shoes were another matter. I turned my room upside down looking for them, but couldn't find them anywhere. Groaning in frustration, I paced about before remembering that the last time I had run was when my shower was broken and my shoes were likely in Nick's old room. Slipping my feet into my shoes, I walked quietly down the stairs, trying not to meet my parents. I didn't want to explain to them why, at almost seventeen, I had changed the habits of a lifetime and got up before nine on a non-school day.

As I walked down to the bottom of the stairs, voices reached me from my father's office and I froze on the steps.

"...be here earlier than expected," came my father's voice.

My mother answered, "I don't understand why?" Her tone made the statement sound like a question and my mind puzzled, trying to figure out the answer.

"It has grown attached and if we don't extract now, then we may not be able to."

"Ah, I see. When will we tell the kids?"

"We'll tell them when we know the date she'll arrive." I could hear them moving outside the door. I was about to lift my foot when the sound of my name made me pause again. "What are we going to do about Nathan?"

"I'm not sure, darling; he's so unlike other boys of this age. When Nick was this age, we were called to the mortal police station twice, had to drag him out of two fights, and he was expelled from school, but Nathan seems so uninterested and detached. Do you think he'll be strong enough to fulfil the role of candidate?"

"He'll have to be! He will not shame my house by being the first male in our line unable to fulfil his destiny as candidate. We'll just need to be harder on him, make him into a man, and ensure that he embraces the Demon in him."

Their voices grew softer as they moved towards the kitchen and I spun around to head back into my room, with their words bouncing around in my head.

By not rebelling and trying to be better than Nick, they were worried about me. Fuck, how could I fix that? Was I able to fix it or would I end up dead like Johan, the last person from our citizens who had been unable to make the sacrifice and had tried to save them. My father had no choice.

I shook my head, grabbed my nearly full water bottle and my iPod from my bag. I plugged the headphones into my ears and decided I needed to take the run. As I neared the stairs, my heart pounded, but no one saw me as I slipped quietly out of the house and ran down the driveway. I ran for five miles and listened to rock music from Nickelback to distract me from any and all thoughts of my parents and them not thinking I could handle being candidate.

I drank some water and ran another ten miles, winding up back at the cliffs we all hung out on. I checked my pockets and realised I'd left my phone on my bed; if anyone had called me, I'd be in deep shit. I needed to shift my ass back home and check to make sure no one needed me for anything.

The run home was short, but I was sweaty when I arrived. I bumped into my sister coming down the stairs. She shook her head in disgust at me as I went past her. In my room, I noticed a note on my bed. I approached with caution, but it was only a reminder that Jack was coming down today and that I had to make up the guest bedroom for him.

I turned the heat on the shower up full and stood under the water, thinking of what to do about the conversation I'd overheard that morning. How could I prove to them that I could perform my duties?

Mortals were nothing to me. I didn't care about them and we did sample them, but we were more careful about it than Nick and his friends were. I hadn't wanted the cops here, especially since we were almost discovered last time, when that girl had been found. She was almost dead and had been screwed by almost all the senior Demon boys in the school. The cops stayed for weeks and my dad went crazy, especially when Nick was interviewed.

I got out of the shower and dried off, and put everything I'd heard to the back of my head so I could get through breakfast like a normal person. After towelling my hair, I wandered downstairs, deciding to make the bed for Jack after I'd eaten. As I walked into the kitchen, I noticed my mother freeze at the cooker.

"Nathan, where were you this morning? I went into your room at seven thirty and you weren't in bed."

"He was out on a run, Mum. I saw him when he came in." I glared at my sister, wondering why she sounded gleeful as I walked towards the breakfast bar for something to eat. My hand reached out for a bagel, but before I could close my hand over one, my mother grabbed my wrist and twisted. I swallowed the shock and pain and looked up at her as she stood over me, glaring down at me.

"Why do you insist on behaving like a mortal, Nathan? There is no need for you to run; you will be fit and healthy as long as you ingest enough luminosity. So why run?" She spoke through her teeth at me, and I honestly didn't know what to say. I enjoyed running; it was a hobby of mine, much like drawing, that kept me sane, especially when I had all these demands on me.

I shook my head, about to answer when her hand twisted my wrist. I couldn't hold back the small pain noise and her eyes widened further. She dropped my wrist, stormed around the table, and grabbed me by the back of my hair, dragging me from the stool and throwing me into the dark room behind the pantry. The door closed with a snap and I breathed a sigh of relief that she hadn't done worse to me, but my relief was short lived.

After a few minutes alone in the dark, the door opened and I knew there was worse to come. I couldn't understand what they wanted from me; we were told to blend in and act like mortals, but when I did, I got shit for it.

"Turn around," my mother's voice commanded. "Hands on the wall!"

My head pounded as I did what she asked and the next second, my t-shirt was moved from the bottom of my back as she touched my skin with the brutally hot fire poker. "You need to remember you're a Demon. You are not a mortal and you need to behave in a manner that does not embarrass your family." The whole time she spoke, slowly enunciating each word, the poker lay across my back and I wanted to scream in agony.

My mind reeled and my back screamed in pain as she moved up and placed it on me again. "Do you understand, Nathan?" I didn't answer straight away. I couldn't process her words because of the pain in my back. One of her hands moved up, grabbed my head, and she whispered with a deadly malice in her voice, "Answer me, Nathan."

Answer her. What the fuck does she want answered?

In the time it took for that to cross my mind, she shoved my head forward and it cracked onto the wall. Stars popped in front of my eyes and my head now throbbed too. She moved the poker and I tried to swallow the whimper of pain as the skin tore away, but I didn't succeed. She placed it again on my lower back and this time when she asked if I understood what I needed to do, I didn't hesitate to answer, "Yes, ma'am."

"You may leave." Her voice came, and as she walked away and left the door open, I crumpled to the floor. I couldn't understand where that had come from. My father had encouraged me to run to help me focus on my duties and at first I had hated it, but then I began to enjoy it and now it was too mortal for me. I retched as the pain in my back scorched and I threw up the water from the run. My back would heal quickly, but that wasn't the point. They wanted someone more Demon than me, and I couldn't figure out how to give them what they wanted.

The next week carried on in the same vein, and as soon as my exams were over, I called my Uncle Jack and asked if I could spend the weekend at his house. The beatings happened weekly and Jack had witnessed first-hand how cruel my parents had gotten when he spotted the burns on my back during a weekend visit. My skin oozed and the blisters burst as I made his bed for the week. He had walked in while I retched into the toilet in his room.

He hadn't said a word to me about it, but I noticed him wince when I was punished because James had hurt a mortal and the police had been involved. The crazy thing was that I didn't think they were punishing me because the police were involved, but because it wasn't me who had involved them. I was almost sure that they wanted me to be the one, the normal demon, who went a little too far with the mortals and got the police involved and I was sure that was why they punished me. Not because someone broke the rules on my watch, but because it wasn't me who disobeyed them.

I left to go to his house a few weeks later and almost sighed in relief when his car pulled into the driveway; the previous night had been particularly brutal. My mum lost it with me because I was in my room listening to my iPod and reading a book on Demon history. She dragged me from my room by my hair and threw me down the stairs, breaking my arm in two places. My dad had healed me, but left the pain as a reminder that I needed to be more Demon-like and stop being such a child.

Uncle Jack's car stopped at the top of the driveway and I walked down the stairs to meet him. He gave me a swift one-armed hug, but glanced down at me in alarm when I winced. He'd hugged my sore side. "Nathan, what happened?" he asked in a low voice, looking at me with concern. "My mother's a psycho who threw me down the fucking stairs."

He shook his head at me as my father stormed out on the porch. He looked in dismay at his younger brother and I saw his eyes tighten as he took in his younger brother's curly brown hair, brown eyes, and tanned skin. My dad was brown-haired like me, with brown eyes like Jack's, and he was tall, taller than Jack. He stalked down the front steps and towered over him.

"What are you doing here, Jack?" he snarled in Jack's face, who glanced up at him in surprise.

"I'm taking the kid here for the weekend, Lewis." The look my dad gave to Jack would have made a weaker man run, but Jack just stared up at him with a cool expression on his face.

"He can't go with you; he has to stay here."

What the fuck? They never had a problem any other time I wanted to stay at Jack's. Hell, they usually pushed me out the door.

"Nathan, go inside." My father's voice commanded, and I turned and strode inside the house, hearing Jack's answer just before I closed the door.

"Lewis, you are going to fucking break that boy. Doing this won't make him more Demon; it'll make him more likely to be the one..."

My dad cut him off, "Be quiet!"

I sat in the kitchen and picked up an apple, watching the clouds darken as rain started to fall in the back garden. The door opened with a creak and my father called me over. "Go and stay at Jack's. Be back here Sunday night for dinner." He turned and walked away. I ran out to the car, jumping in and closing the door.

Jack turned to me and said, "Listen, kid, I know they are fucked up, but believe it or not, they are trying to do what is best for you." I just nodded, not for one second believing what he said, but knowing I somehow had to find a way to be more Demon. Jack would help me. I trusted him and he was always there for me when I needed him.

"Jack, what were you like as a boy?" I asked curiously.

He laughed before answering, "Which time?" and I looked at him sourly. "Okay, okay. I get it. I was a little shit, my parents had me tied to that fucking tree almost every week. I rebelled against them, dating mortal girls, drinking underage. Hell, one night, I convinced my mate's fiancé to... Well, maybe you don't need to know that story, but I was trouble. I still am." He finished with a grin and I smiled at the thought that I needed to be more like Jack.

He turned on the radio and the rest of the four-hour car journey to Leeds passed quickly. We joked around and he told me stories about what my dad was like while my grandparents still walked among us. We finally reached his cottage and decided to go to the pub down the road for dinner and a few pints. He let me have two pints and then took me back to his house, with the promise of fishing the next day.

"Wake up, sunshine." Jack's voice woke me from a disturbing sleep where I dreamed about redness again. "We're going fishing today." I groaned and he brought me in a cup of coffee and a bagel, placing them on the dresser beside me. "Come on, if you're not up in ten minutes. I'm leaving your ass here."

I sipped the coffee while getting dressed and eating the bagel in the car. The day was overcast and thankfully dry as we headed to Swillington Park for some fishing. We fished at three different lakes; the first one wasn't giving us anything. The second had a dog splashing around, but the third was quiet and we caught a few fish. It was fun until the skies opened and a bolt of lightning hit the tree opposite us.

We got back to the car and made small talk on the way back to his house. "You got a girl yet, Nate?" His voice probed me and I answered without thinking, "No, net yet, Jack. But there is a girl I have my eye on." He looked questioningly at me from the corner of his eye when I didn't elaborate.

"Demon?" he asked curiously. I nodded and thought about how I did like a girl in school, but asking her out was difficult; she was one of my sister's besties and I didn't really want a clingy-assed girl hanging off my arm.

"She's one of Jenny's friends, Lisa." He nodded at her name and I knew he knew who she was. "I like her, but I'm not sure I wanna date her." I answered Jack honestly and he laughed.

"More fuck em and chuck em, eh?" I laughed with him and at that

11

moment, I realised he'd helped me to figure out that I could be happy as a Demon as long as I embraced it and didn't take my life too seriously.

The weekend at Jack's helped me clear my head and I came back determined to become more Demon than ever. I started fucking with their minds at school and only Joe seemed surprised at me leading it. I sampled more and my powers grew, but the beating continued.

CHAPTER 2
DISCO SURPRISES

She was hot, tall, slim, and blond, with big tits and a nice ass. Her eyes were this deep blue, almost violet and she seemed to like me. Plus, she was from another Demon family so my folks would like it. At the school disco, I had decided to make a move on her and as soon as I walked in, I made a beeline for her, grabbing her hand and pulling her up to dance. I was the Chiefs's son and no one said no to me. She leaned up and whispered in my ear, "I've wanted this for a while. I'm so glad you picked me."

Her words turned me on and I grabbed her hand, pulling her out of the dining hall where the disco was being held. We reached the doors and saw innocent little Danni walking into the school with some of her friends. I smirked and looked over at Lisa, noticing her smile brighten as I nodded over at the girls.

She nodded in response and we walked over to the girls, clamouring the others to walk away and leave Danni behind. Danni froze as we reached her. I took her hand and whispered into her ear that everything was fine; she was just coming with us for a little bit.

We walked along until we found an open classroom. Three or four were always left open for occasions such as tonight, because we, as Demons, were allowed to sample the mortals as long as we left them mostly unharmed. Mortals were good for helping us feel high, but not as good as sacrifices on Halloween were.

Closing the door softly behind us, I turned as Lisa led Danni over to sit on the teacher's desk. She told her to stay, walked over, and kissed me almost violently. My cock twitched as she snaked her hand behind my head and I groaned into her mouth as she pressed her hot little body closer to my own.

I kissed down her neck and pulled her over to the wall by the door. Her chest made my mouth water as I watched her nipples harden, waiting for me to play with her tits. I wet my fingers and slipped my hand up to play with one nipple, while my teeth nipped on her lips and my hand knotted itself in her hair. Knowing we had a mortal audience to this was even more of a turn on. I moved her closer to the desk, and kissed down her neck and back up to her lips as she panted in my ear.

She leaned back on the desk and I slipped my fingers up her skirt, grazing her clit. She growled up at me as I touched her through her underwear. "Nathan, oh my God." I smiled and turned towards Danni. She sat staring straight ahead and Lisa groaned as I moved towards Danni. She sat up and fixed her top, sliding down from the desk and standing opposite me. We shared a glance, nodded, and turned our Demon side on. Faces elongating and rough, eyes turning to purple with our heightened desire. Lips became rough and teeth became sharp and black. I licked my lips and used my fingers, turned into claws, to slice a little cut on Danni's shoulder. Sucking in her luminosity felt amazing, but I knew we couldn't take too much; otherwise, we would drain her. It was so difficult to stop.

My breath stuttered as I pulled away, and growled at Lisa. "That's enough." She didn't respond as I ran my finger back up Danni's shoulder, healing her, and walked over to Lisa. I grabbed her and pulled her off, healing the other side as Lisa hit me repeatedly on the chest. Ignoring her, I turned my attention to Danni. "Go back to the dance and remember that you broke your shoe. You rushed home and changed into a different pair."

As she left, I turned towards Lisa and moved with the predator inside me in control. I backed her into the wall and took her lip between my teeth, running my hands up and down her arms, pulling her closer to me as I finally kissed her. I pushed her legs apart and lifted her slightly off the floor, resting her over my throbbing cock. I was just about to pull her top down again when the door banged open.

I turned towards the door and James stood there, with a look beyond loathing on his face as he took us in. Joe walked up behind him. James shrugged him off, storming away and crashing through the door at the bottom of the corridor.

"Lisa, I need to have a word with Nate." Joe's voice sounded apologetic.

"Can't it wait mate?" I asked him with a bite to my voice, groaning a little as Lisa ground on my cock.

"No, it can't. Lisa, fuck off."

She pushed me away and stormed out of the room, glaring at Joe as she barged into his shoulder as she passed. Joe burst out laughing and walked into the room, while I fixed the bulge in my trousers. "This better be fucking important, Joe."

"I know, man. I would never normally burst in on you, but this shit needs to be dealt with and you need to do it."

"We'll, what the fuck is it?" I walked towards him and he moved. I followed him, curious about why he'd felt the need to give me a serious case of blue balls. Walking was uncomfortable as I waited for my boner to go down, but I knew Joe. It had to have been something serious to interrupt a Demon rite of passage. As Demons matured, we were granted by the council a few rites of passage and fucking our chosen in the school after a sampling was seen as a good way to create more Demons, a way of binding us to our future partners.

We walked through the swinging doors and reached a wide open classroom door. Jenny and Swinson were in a heavy make-out session. This bothered me because he was a mate and she was a fucking nightmare of a Demon bitch. She might be my sister, but she was like a fucking snake. Strike first; ask later. I looked over at Joe questioningly; although I didn't like Jenny fucking around with one of my mates, I wasn't able to stop her.

As he pointed into the room, I saw three mortals lying on the floor, barely moving. I moved towards them and my lineage took over as I turned towards my friend and my sister. "STOP NOW!" I commanded in a high clear voice. Jenny froze and Swinson swung round to face me with his dick standing at attention, and on full display.

"What the fuck did yous do?" I asked as I leaned over the mortals. "They are nearly drained." Swinson made a move towards me, but his cock still swung free. "For fuck sake, man, put it away, will you."

Jenny glared at me. "We were just having some fun." She smirked at my expression and walked out the door, leaving me with my friends, one of whom I wanted to murder.

He walked over and bent down beside me. I reared back, punching him full on in the face. "Don't fuck my sister in the school." I whispered at him maliciously.

He nodded at me, uttering an apology as we roused the mortals and healed them. We told them they had been taking drugs and had collapsed in school. We took them back to the dining hall, telling the staff that we had found them lying in one of the classrooms passed out. Only the Demon teachers were suspicious, but they let it go when they realised that the samples were going to be okay.

After answering a few questions, I looked about for Lisa and found her over with her friends. I moved towards her and Joe caught my arm. "Nate, are you sure about her? She's a fucking live wire and she'll eat you alive."

Laughing off his concern, I walked towards Lisa and she smiled at my approach. It wasn't every day the Chiefs's son wanted to date, so she lapped it up. I finally reached her and asked her to meet me the next day at the cliffs. She nodded and I left smiling for a change. My smile didn't last long as Joe caught up with me outside.

"Did you know Lisa came with James?" I shrugged and shook my head no as it clicked into place why he had looked so pissed off earlier. He would just have to suck it up. I outranked him, so she was mine.

"He's gonna make your life a misery, Nate. You know what he's like; he doesn't like to share."

"He won't be fucking sharing."

Joe looked at me sideways, but I couldn't read his expression. He nodded once, before walking away and leaving me. I was about to shout after him when my phone beeped in my pocket. It was a text from Lisa.

I can't wait for tomorrow. Hopefully, we can finish what we started.
Lisa

Grinning while I typed,

Me either and I hope so too. You need me to pick you up or can you find
your way to the clearing at the cliffs? N

I accidentally sent it to her and Joe and I laughed when Joe text me back.

Na, mate. I'm just not into you.

Lisa's reply followed quickly as she told me her address and asked what time to pick her up. I walked home in a good mood, whistling along the path, but I should have known the good feeling wouldn't last long.

Even though I acted more Demon than ever, I was booted into the dark room for the night. When I awoke the next morning, my good mood had vanished.

CHAPTER 3
DATING PROBLEMS

I sat in the cinema with Lisa. She bugged me and I tuned her out, staring at the screen thinking about the sacrifice. I knew It was scum and that it shouldn't even cross my mind, but something about it scared me. My thoughts were worrying because It wasn't even due for a number of months yet, and I bet my brother never had these thoughts when his first sacrifice arrived. I wasn't sure whether it would be a male or a female sacrifice this year, although it was normally a girl since they were the most powerful — their luminosity was brighter than that of a male and more sustaining.

"Nate," Lisa whined in my ear, dragging me away from my thoughts.

"What's up, babe?" I asked. I wanted to feel as attracted to her as I used to and wondered why I needed to force myself to feel something, anything for her. When we had first started dating a few months ago, I couldn't keep my hands off her; it was as if I was consumed with desire.

"I'm hungry," she said, raising her eyes suggestively at the people in front of us, a college-aged guy and girl, probably only a few years older than we were. I smiled and pushed my emotions to the side as I felt my face change to that of a predator. We nodded at each other, leaned forward, and slit a hole through the back of their necks.

As the first hit of blood and essence hit the back of my throat, I groaned. Her hand rubbed my thigh, inching upwards, but just as she reached where I was desperate for her to touch, we were thrown back against the seat. As we struggled to come back to reality, my father's voice echoed in our ears.

"Stop now! If you do not, you will both be exiled." We panted in frustration as we made our way out of the cinema. I shook, on a major high, and she giggled like a maniac.

After stumbling a few steps along the road, I pushed her down an alley and kissed her ferociously until my father's voice echoed in my head.

"That's enough! Nathan, come home now." I sighed and kissed her again before I headed home to deal with whatever punishment would be enforced.

The closer I walked towards home, the more I came down from the high, fearing what lay ahead until I began shaking as I reached the door. I took a deep breath as my father walked towards me, his movements swift and calculated.

"You have to be more careful, son. We can't have our world exposed because you can't control your urges."

He searched my face for a moment before walking back into his office. He closed the door while I watched him, stunned. My father usually punished me for one indiscretion or another, and this was a pretty large rule to have broken. I couldn't believe my luck and took off to my room before he changed his mind.

That was the first night I ever dreamed of her. Her glossy brown hair framed her innocent face, so sweetly it left me breathless. Her beguiling eyes were deep hazel and made me want to sell my soul for one real moment with her. She stood surrounded by mist at a distance from me and stared. Our eyes connected and we drank each other in as the atmosphere crackled with desperation. She took slow deliberate steps towards me, only stopping when our noses almost touched and I could taste her sweet breath in the air. "Save me, Nathan," she whispered and vanished. I jumped awake, panic and frustration coursing through me.

I couldn't get back to sleep, tossing and turning all night long. My heart pounded every time I pictured her perfect face and my palms began to sweat. This was a new feeling to me; I hadn't felt anything like this yearning before.

Throughout the following day, I struggled with tiredness. I couldn't concentrate in class. My brain wasn't working properly. I sat in class and the teachers constantly questioned us, but I struggled to keep my eyes open. I was stumped when one of my teachers asked me a question. I hadn't been listening at all. My whole being focused on her face and when I looked down, I had been doodling on my jotter, drawing her face over and over. I saw this girl everywhere I looked, in reflections on the window and in the corridors, but when I tried to catch her, she would vanish. It really messed with my head.

I wasn't interested in Lisa. I didn't want to see my friends or do any of the things I normally did. It was normally fun to mess with the mortals around us and make them see or feel things that weren't real. It gave us no end of amusement and we all usually laughed when they flipped out and ran into trees or tripped over rocks. It wasn't enough to distract me. Joe noticed. He was my best friend and had been since I was two. He knew me well enough to spot something was amiss.

"Nate, what's up, mate? You seem really distant."

"Huh? Sorry, I missed that."

"I said what's up?"

I looked at my friend and wondered what to tell him. Luckily, he asked me a question that would get me out of telling him about her; it seemed crazy to dream about a girl I had never met.

"Is it because you're the dude with the knife, their candidate?"

"Yeah, man. I don't wanna freak out or anything, but it worries me. I mean, I know we're monsters, but actually driving the knife in... I'm scared I'll do it wrong or mess up. I keep worrying that something's gonna go wrong..." *Or my dream girl would show up*. I finished that thought in my head, worried that Joe would think I was going soft. Demons weren't supposed to have feelings like that or worry, but sometimes I couldn't help it. Joe watched me with a worried expression and when he spoke, it was in a lower voice than normal.

"It's okay; it'll be fine. I'm sure most candidates for Ascension go through this. Don't stress, mate." I nodded and walked along, unable to get the girl out of my mind. It fascinated me but I had to let go and focus on my life.

I looked around and spotted a few of the mortal girls in our year. My mind battled with indecision, but after a beat, I decided to toy with them. I hoped this would cheer me up, but I wasn't feeling too optimistic.

Danni, was right in my line of sight. I forced my way into her mind, wincing at the images. I saw her with James, him kissing her, him toying with her. It made me seethe. I hated that fucker. He thought he was something because of his father and he treated mortals like dirt. If he hurt another one, I would end him. We couldn't have mortals getting hurt at random. The police would descend on our world and cause chaos. I changed her mind about him, forcing her to change her feelings about him to distrust and dislike.

I focused in on the part of her brain I needed. Moving through the halls of our school and I concentrated hard as I altered her mind. In her head, I found the perfect fear — spiders. I put the image of spiders running across the floor into her mind and suddenly she looked down, screaming and crying. She swiped her arms across her chest, her breath coming in short gasps.

Her friends all looked at her in shock as she began shaking when she saw one spider, then another, climbing up her body. She screamed again and stumbled backwards. Her friends were frantic as they tried to calm her down.

"Danni? What's wrong?"

"There's nothing there, sweetie."

Danni looked right at me. Her eyes were wide with terror as she patted down her body repeatedly. Her heart hammered, her breathing became more challenging, and she leaned against the wall with tears rolling down her cheeks. The boys passing by snickered and shouted things.

"Jeeso, someone let you out of the asylum early."

"What *is* wrong with you?"

I felt a deep sense of shame, the game that normally made me feel better had lost its appeal. I averted my eyes as we passed her on our way into the dining hall. My friends all laughed raucously, but I couldn't stop myself from glancing back. She still stood with tears streaming down her cheeks and the feeling of shame burned through me again. *What had I just done? Why was this even an issue for me now?*

As I sat with my friends, I felt sick, but distracted myself by starting a conversation with Lucca and Swinson about the candidacy. When lunch ended, I felt happier and more relaxed as I went to my afternoon classes.

After school, I was walking home when James knocked into my shoulder and almost sent me sprawling.

"Whoops! Sorry, candidate," he said derisively before he walked away sniggering. I wanted to go after him and rip him limb from limb. I took a few calming breaths and thought to myself. *What would be the point in going after him?* He was an idiot trying to goad me because someone let slip that if I couldn't carry out the candidacy then he'd be next in line. The thought of that sadistic prick killing anyone scorched through me. I needed to make sure he wouldn't be able to hold himself up, never mind direct a knife at anyone.

The closer I got to home, the more I felt like a complete idiot. *Why did I feel shame over a stupid mortal? That had never happened to me before, so why now? What had changed?* As my thoughts raced through my head, the only thing I could think of clearly was the girl in my dream. She was all that had changed and it unnerved me that, even hours later, I could still picture her face as clear as day in my mind.

CHAPTER 4
IN THE DARKNESS

Three weeks after the unnerving taste of humanity, my parents told us we were getting a new foster child. This meant their next sacrifice would arrive quicker than we had expected. The thought didn't bother me at all now. My humanity was once again back where it belonged, buried in my mind. I half-listened to what they said — a girl would be coming. The girl was almost seventeen and would be here for a whole year, but she would be placed under an enchantment to stop her from noticing our powers and our Demon sides.

Sacrifices were brought to Halloween because their luminosity sustained our Demon side and fed the darkness in our souls. The powers they possessed transferred mostly into the candidates that year, but also strengthened the Demon populace. I mulled this over while my father watched me. He stared at me in that detached way of his.

"Nathan, as our candidate for the next four years, you will be the one to take her powers in." His mouth drew to a thin line as he watched me absorb the information. "She is one of the most powerful sacrifices we have ever had and we are extracting her early due to her becoming attached to her current foster family. It will be your duty to watch her; caring for her will make her soul brighter and her powers more intense. You will be one of the most powerful people on our Council of Superiors. Do not disappoint me. An edict will be passed forbidding others from hurting her and I will personally deal with the punishments of those who break the edict."

His words rang with warning and Jenny shivered at the malice in his voice. She wasn't used to hearing it like I was. He usually spoke to me this way and I usually avoided direct confrontation with my parents. All I ever saw when my father looked at me was disappointment, but what disappointed him, I wasn't sure. I looked away from my parents and focused on a bug crawling up the window frame until my father cleared his voice, drawing my eyes back to him. The usual disappointment was replaced with anger as he stared at me, scalding and holding me in place. "Do you understand your role, Nathan?" I shrugged, watching with interest as his eyes widened at my small display of dissension.

He ignored me as he continued speaking through a tight smile. "Mortals, especially sacrifices enflame our kind and cause fighting and discord. You will notice extreme reactions from our friends, but since she is our tribute, we are protected by the enchantment I'll place on her as soon as she arrives." He paused and his eyes swept the table, landing on me again, "Nathan, do you understand what I'm telling you?"

I glanced over at him and his face hardened as he looked at me. I bit out my answer, "Of course I do. I'm not fucking stupid."

Wow, way to go, Nate. Flip the fuck out and cause a riot at another family meeting.

My dad glared at me and growled, "Show a little respect to me and your mother, Nathan."

I shook my head at the comment, trying to control the discontent I felt with my family, but my mother took it to mean my refusal.

"Clear the room," my mother snapped. My father shook his head, and he and my sister moved out of the room without a backward glance. My mother flew out of her seat, the sound clattering to the floor was all I could hear as my heart pounded loudly in my ears.

Oh fuck, what had I just done?

My eyes closed of their own volition, but I opened them quickly as my mother stormed around the breakfast bar towards me. She grabbed me roughly by the shoulders, threw me to the floor, and stood towering above me. She looked at me in disgust. "You will learn your place, Nathan, and you will learn to respect me and your father or you'll regret it. Do you understand?" I nodded again, noting the rising colour in her cheeks and her quickening breath. I knew what was coming as she dragged me across the floor to the hidden room. I knew because she usually dragged me in here to punish me at least once a month for one indiscretion or another.

The room was pitch black, dank, and musty, and the only light was from a slither coming in the open doorway. Looking over at the wall, I wanted to panic and wriggle, but stopped myself. The more I freaked out, the more severe the punishment would be. She dragged me to the rope on the wall, tied my hands to it, and left. I tried to slow my breathing down, but it sped up again when I realised she'd left the door ajar. *Oh fuck, that meant she was coming back.* It also meant my father's belt hanging by the door wasn't brutal enough for this. What was she going to use now, a whip? The last time I was whipped flashed into my mind, the pain of the lashes lasting days and the burning as each lash hit.

My heart raced and my breathing sped as I remembered how careful they were not to hit me where anyone would see it. Not that she minded them seeing their brutality, but they didn't want people to know I was unruly. I closed my eyes and tried to calm myself down, but as soon as I heard the footsteps outside the door, my heart raced even faster. Blood rushed into my ears and blocked out the sound of her approach. I was sweating so much that my t-shirt stuck to my skin.

Suddenly there was a whistling sound followed by a burning sensation. My body tensed in pain and I realised her weapon of choice was the cane. It hit me again and again, but no sound escaped me. I gulped down my screams of agony. I knew they would make her hit me more so I kept quiet, feeling tears running down my face and my chest heaving as I struggled to keep it all in.

Eventually my head went limp on my arms. She walked out and left me without a word. My legs felt like jelly. I shook and shivered for what felt like years. I kept seeing the girl's face as though she haunted me in the darkness. My eyes stung as my tears fell. *Why did I keep pissing them off? Was there something I had done to annoy them so much that I deserved this?*

After a while, the scorching of my back and aching arms distracted me from my thoughts. My head swam and although unconsciousness beckoned me, I knew I couldn't succumb, because if they came back and I was unconscious, there would be hell to pay.

A short while later, my parents came in together. My father stopped just inside the door. I heard the sound of metal scraping over the hook at the door as my father picked up the belt. My heart rate jumped up furiously and my breaths stuttered. My body froze as one fact penetrated my mind. I was about to be beaten again.

The room was so dark I could barely make him out. The belt flew through the air with a whistle before cracking on the skin on my back. I couldn't help it this time — I cried out as he hit my already raw skin. He hit me repeatedly until I blacked out from the agony.

I awoke hours later, struggling against the ropes. My arms were on fire and I couldn't focus on anything, not even her face, which swam in front of my blurry vision time and again. I swam in and out of my pain for what felt like forever, alone in the darkness with no light at all.

The door opened and I flinched, but my mother came over towards me and softly wiped the sweat from my forehead. She didn't say a thing to me as she untied the ropes from my arms and walked out of the room. The door closed as I crumpled in a heap on the floor. I didn't remember falling asleep, but I awoke to the sound of someone in the room with me. I sat up and as I moved, the skin on my back felt worn down to the bone. I swallowed a groan of agony and didn't move again. I didn't think I could take another beating like the previous night, but it was just Jenny bringing me in a tray of food and water. She looked at me in disgust as she moved closer and I tried to sit a little straighter.

"Why do you antagonise them, Nathan? What's going on with you?" I said nothing, but shook my head, my body protesting violently at the movement. She lit a match and touched it to a large, round white candle, my first indication that I would be in the room for a while.

The light touched upon my hands and they were caked in blood. The rope had ripped my skin off and blood covered my arms and fingers. I reached my arm out to grab some food but the movement caused my back to seize up and I almost went under again. Not reacting, Jenny moved out of the room, leaving me with my food and only a candle to see. I sat there trying to encourage myself to move and eventually managed to take a few sips of water. I managed to eat half a sandwich, even though every movement sent fire roaring through me.

The cool wall soothed my burning back as I waited for an indiscriminate amount of time for the door to open, and my dad to come in. He normally did, with some balm and some charm to speed up the healing process, but nobody came. I became delirious with the pain, seeing visions and daydreams. I couldn't figure out what they were or what they meant, but they helped me escape the darkness and I welcomed them.

In the first one, the girl ran and fell over at my feet, staring up at me. Her eyes spoke to my soul, but I ignored them, feeling more powerful than ever before. All I could feel was the power coursing through my veins. I stood there, straight and proud, and drew the knife across her throat, her arms, and down her chest.

In the delusion, I lapped the blood and shook while glowing white hot. I could feel the heat radiating from somewhere deep inside me and the power of it made me feel drunk and lightheaded.

Without warning, the vision shifted and I saw myself kissing the girl, stroking her hair while she cradled a baby in her arms, one with my eyes and my hair colour, but her full lips and thick hair. With a sudden bang, I saw my parents stalk in, going after her and the baby and I screamed undecipherable words. I awoke in a sweat, cursing under my breath; my heart still raced and the sweat made my back burn. The pain made me wretch and I vomited over my arms and legs as I tried without success to calm my heart rate down. I vomited again and this time closed my eyes, leaning my head against the cool wall. I waited, but for what I didn't know.

The girl's face swam again in my vision and out of the darkness came the desire to protect her, unbidden but stronger than anything I had ever felt before in my life. I knew I would give my life for this girl if I ever had the chance to.

Finally, the door opened and my parents walked into the room with Jenny, pausing in disgust at the pool of sick. They came towards me as I squinted at them, blinking in the bright light streaming in from the doorway behind them.

"Have you learned your lesson?" My father asked with malice in his voice and I knew no matter my answer, this wouldn't be over. I started to answer but he punched me in the jaw, cracking my head off the wall. Lights popped in front of my vision and the door slammed shut before I could focus on anything or say a single word.

I sat in the darkening room and watched the candlelight burn lower and lower, taking all my willpower with it. The pain became more intense and I put my head into my hands even though this caused my back to burn in agony. Tears rolled down my cheeks and I swiped them away, angry with myself for betraying such a human emotion. I shook all over and my body was covered with a sheen of sweat, prompting licks of fire to dance up and down my back.

Unable to move, my breathing came in short, sharp gasps. I slipped under again, only waking up as I was pulled to my feet. My brother, back from university, was on one side of me, and my sister on the other. They half-pulled, half-dragged me to the stairs. Jenny's face paled as she took in the bloody mess that was my back.

They couldn't touch it, I almost blacked out when they tried and each attempt drew a high-pitched yelp from me. The noises I made sounded as though they came from a wounded animal instead of a human being. They both took an arm and eventually we made it up the stairs. My back burned as blood flowed down it.

As we reached my room, my vision turned black at the edges and I stumbled more and more. I collapsed on the floor by my bed, gasping for breath as my head spun. Nick groaned as he pulled me back up and I made that yelping sound again as agony shot through me. He paused as he lay me down on the bed, cursing under his breath at the sight of my mangled back.

We all knew Dad could heal it, but he obviously enjoyed my suffering since he didn't offer to help.

As I drifted out of consciousness, I listened to my brother and sister conversing in terse whispers behind me, "Jesus, Jenny, look at the state of his back. What the fuck did he do to deserve that?"

"He was disrespectful, not answering questions and shrugging like our lives and traditions were of little interest to him and..."

"Oh, for fuck sake, you are actually going to defend that? Surely if it was just a punishment, Dad would have healed him by now. No, he's sending a message and using his own son to do it. I'm going back to uni tonight. I won't stay in this house while they are on a power trip like this."

I heard retreating footsteps and a huff before my door closed over. I was left lying face down on my bed, unable to move at all. After a few hours, I felt strong enough to move. I swung my legs over the bed as I pushed myself up with my hands. I gasped aloud, but forced myself to stand on shaky legs until I collapsed on the floor again. I started crawling to the bathroom. Before I made it halfway, my bedroom door opened and my parents stood there watching me crawl across the floor on my knees.

Both of them stalked in and dragged me back towards the bed, causing tears of frustration to leak from my eyes. They threw me down on my bed on my back and I screamed in agony. I looked at them through my swimming vision, but my ears rang so loudly that I couldn't hear what they said to me. I knew better than to ask.

I nodded along to what they were saying, which got me punched in the head again. My vision spotted as they stormed out of my room, leaving me on my bed feeling more alone and confused than ever. I rolled over onto my back and tried to control my breathing.

I could hear raised voices in the hall. My father yelled after Nick before I heard a door slam shut and storming footsteps, getting louder and louder. My door opened with a crash and I glanced over to see my father glaring at me in a rage. He moved towards me and I shrank back, sinking into the bed as he reached me and loosened his belt.

I couldn't move as he hit me again and again, not on my back this time

29

but across my butt cheeks and down my legs. The pain was unbearable and I screamed into my pillow before my vision clouded over black and I drifted off into a hallucination with her again.

In the vision, she didn't even look at me and I found myself desperate for some way to connect with her. I reached out to touch her hair, but she disappeared before I could reach her. I panicked and saw her ahead of me in the woods, our woods outside. I ran towards her through a bonfire, not caring that my body was on fire. The flames burned my back, but I was completely consumed with reaching her. After a few moments, I caught up with her in the clearing and she whispered to me.

"Save me, Nathan. Please." Her voice sounded desperate and as her eyes looked into mine, I could see tears form and run down her cheeks. I reached out to wipe away a tear, but just as my hand grazed her face, she vanished. A wraith appeared in the spot she had been standing in.

The wraith moved towards me and I ran blindly, stumbling over rocks and branches. Suddenly I fell down the main stairs in our school. The wraith drew nearer to me and as I thudded onto the landing at the bottom of the steps, I awoke. I tried to turn over onto my back, but yelped and spun back onto my front as the mattress grated my back.

I lay there for hours with my eyes open. The pain became nothing more than a meaningless blur as I focused my thoughts on getting to the bathroom. I ignored the fire scorching through me as I stumbled across my room. I shut myself in for a few moments, trying to calm my pounding heart and gasping breaths. Once I had managed to calm myself down, I relieved myself and went back to my bed. I gingerly sat on the edge of the bed and fell asleep sitting up with my head pressed against the headboard.

As I slowly awoke, I realised it must have been Saturday or Sunday since I hadn't been awakened for school. I wasn't sure; I felt like I had been in the dark room for weeks, not just a day or two. I looked around for my phone, desperate to find out what day it was when my father walked in. He barely glanced at me hunched against the headboard as he stalked over to me. He spoke to me in a louder voice than normal, the sounds bouncing around my head as the pain reared its ugly head again.

"I think by now you have learned your lesson. Turn around. Know this, Nathan. I will not tolerate disrespect from you or anyone else. I will not heal your whole body as a reminder to you that you need to learn your place among us." He moved his hands up and down my back and the pain receded until it was only a dull ache in most areas except for a throbbing burn left on my lower back. "Go for a shower. We have a council meeting in half an hour and I expect you to be there, well presented and on time. You will make your own way there." He got up and walked towards the door, turning back only to throw me one last glance. "If you are late, I will undo the relief and you will find yourself back in your world of pain. "

With that, he slammed the door closed. I stood slowly, stiffening as where he had left the pain burned and I realised it was right at the bottom of my back. I grimaced as I realised that any trousers I wore would irritate the life out of me as they rubbed against the sensitive skin.

I moved into the bathroom and looked at myself in the mirror. My wrists were still red raw, rubbed by the ropes. My face was bruised and bloody, and the little I could see of my back was a mess, big black bruises over scabbing skin and loose bits floating around, barely attached. This shower would hurt so badly. I almost wanted to give it a miss, but I knew I needed to clean up, especially if there was a council meeting that I had to attend.

I turned the water on, leaving the heat down low and stepped in. My skin caught fire and I pounded on the wall as my whole body felt incinerated by the water. I was so consumed by the pain that when her face swam into my mind, it distracted me and helped dull the pain like a panacea. I washed as best I could and headed to my bedroom, where I found clothes already laid out on my bed. Alongside the clothes, I saw a tonic with a note attached.

Nathan,

Drink this tonic to help with the bruising.

Mum

My mum had left me a long-sleeved white t-shirt, jeans, a belt, and a jumper. My mother was one sadistic bitch. The jeans she had picked sat high on my waist right where the beating remained and the jumper was heavy and stiff, which meant I would have to wriggle to get it on, but I didn't dare refuse. *How could I?* I knew exactly what would happen to me if I did.

I ran down the stairs, wincing with every step as my jeans irritated the raw skin. It wasn't long until I felt the trickle of sticky wetness that showed I was bleeding. I tried my best to ignore the pain as I ran, stopping once to retch into the flowerbed outside the meeting hall. I entered with only moments to spare, out of breath from running and struggling with the pain. I met my father's sharp gaze as he stood beside the sanctuary and I knew I'd have to stay for the whole meeting, even though non-council members were usually dismissed halfway through.

CHAPTER 5
THE MEETING

I entered the church and walked down the aisles. My eyes were trained on the sanctuary where the Council of Superiors sat. My father sat at the head of the table, directly below the stained glass window, which was a thing of beauty — a cross with various colours of blue in the background with vines wrapping around it, grapes at the top and dove flying overhead. I had always loved to watch the way the light trickled through and lit the place.

I looked around as I walked towards our row at the front of the disused church, trying to see things from a different perspective. The most important families occupied the top four rows of wooden benches, over two aisles and each four rows represented the importance of their families or their involvement with the Superiors or the Chief. As the candidate this year, I would eventually take a place on the council, but wouldn't be allowed the deciding vote on issues or motion for any changes of circumstances. If it came to me to be the deciding party, my mother as the Chief's wife would have the vote.

The walls of the church were caramel in colour and even though the place hadn't been used in years, it still smelled of incense and candles. The benches were wooden with red kneeling boards but there was no religious paraphernalia on the walls. All images of Christianity had been stripped out, with the exception of the stained glass window and little crosses ingrained in the glass and the wooden panels that lined the walls every few feet.

There were four sets of benches each with an aisle down them, but the biggest was the one I headed down towards my family, none of whom turned to look at me, or even acknowledge my arrival.

I took my allotted seat and spotted some of my friends. As they walked towards me, I shook my head slightly at them, warning them not to come near me. Joe was quickest on the uptake, though he glanced at me quizzically and dragged them back to their seats. I perched on the edge of the bench, trying my best to control my breathing and racing heart.

Lisa walked in and my stomach churned; she would be sure to ask questions. I knew that if she touched me, I'd probably either break her jaw or rip her to shreds. My father stopped her from coming near me, pointing instead at my sister. Since he was the Chief, no one would ever dare to say no.

Nick slumped down beside me. "I see you were finally given a break?" he probed. I nodded at him, not wanting to speak to him or anyone else in our family yet.

I watched as James sauntered into the hall and saw him smarm up to my dad before turning towards me, smirking.

"I hate that prick," I muttered, not quite under my breath and Nick turned towards me in alarm.

"Why?" he almost whispered. He didn't quite manage to keep it under his breath.

"He's a sadistic prick. He keeps hinting that he's gonna take my candidacy position at the feast. I wanna stab him in the face and watch the light fade from his eyes as I tear him limb from limb." Nick looked at me in stunned silence until I asked, "What?"

"Nothing, you're just more like Dad than I expected."

I bristled at the thought, then realised it wasn't such a bad thing since one day, I would be a leader of an assembly like this. There were much worse things I could be than my father. He garnered respect and no one questioned his judgement or his rulings.

The first half of the meeting passed in a blur of proposals, adjournments, and denied motions. I only paid attention to half of it, although as a candidate, I was supposed to listen to all parts regarding Transference, but I mostly tuned them out. I didn't want to think about being the Transference candidate when all it had gotten me so far were beatings and more pain than I wanted.

I began people watching for most of the meeting, seeing her face wherever I looked. It unnerved me. I was lost in thought about her when a sharp poke in my ribs made me pay attention. I glanced at my brother from the corner of my eye and saw him nodding towards the sanctuary. I stood immediately and began the slow walk up the sanctuary steps towards my father. My legs shook and I worried about what I would face. Only the most major of indiscretions would have me hauled up into the sanctuary and in our two thousand year history, only two people, aside from Transference candidates, were ever called up. As soon as that thought crossed my mind, I felt like an idiot. *How could I not have realised what I was going up for?*

I glanced around the church as I continued the short walk and noticed Lisa watching me with a smile on her lips. I responded in kind, but focused on what I would face. I sucked in a deep breath as I forced a calm I didn't really feel. I moved closer and smiled at the Superiors. Starting with the least important members, I made my way along the table shaking the Superiors' hands. After each handshake, they turned towards the table, cutting themselves with the ceremonial dagger and placing six droplets of blood into the Vessel. The Vessel and the Ceremonial Blade were passed to each member as I moved along the table. When I reached my father, I was almost sick with nerves at the sight of him standing up from the end of the table with the blade in his hand. He watched my eyes widen and the creepiest smile I had ever seen appeared on his mouth. He shook my hand, turned from me, and cut his hand, keeping the Ceremonial Blade in his hand as he took a sip from the Vessel.

The Vessel was gold with rubies in a circle round the rim and the handle. It was a sacred Vessel, one that we used on Halloween during the Transference feast. The Vessel was then passed back from Superior to Superior, then onto the wives before making its way back towards me. My whole body shook as my mother walked towards us holding the cup. Her eyes were glacial and she didn't smile at me or give any sign that I was her child. She handed the cup to my father and turned away, heading back to her seat without even a glance in my direction.

It was my Inauguration ceremony and my father hadn't told me it was happening. Inauguration meant I was officially a candidate. James, Lucca, and Swinson were all the backups for my candidacy and if I failed, the next on the list would take over. They all stood beside their families and if I hadn't been so self-absorbed, I would have perhaps noticed them before I was called up. As the Vessel was about to be passed to me, I noticed a derisive smirk on James' face and my hands began to shake. My father conveyed the ritual for Inauguration, "Son, on this day, you will become our Transference candidate. It will be your role to lead our people this year until four years from today. You will be expected to display our ideals at all times, remain aloof from mortals, and protect your sacrifice's luminosity. Do you accept?"

Looking at him in this capacity, he seemed benign, but behind his brown eyes a fire roared.

"I do." I answered respectfully.

"Recite after me:

In times of old, we stood alone, breaking back and hauling stone,

We fought for blood and valour free, dreaming of a time we'd see,

The fruits of labours tall and slim, souls devoured, lives within,

Hunger ending, lives depending, mortal essences unending.

I will protect, I will not falter, all my life I serve the alter,

Protect the order and rise with rigour all."

I recited the words, feeling proud and brave, and smiled as my father handed me the Vessel. He nodded, smiling at me as I drank the blood of my Demon Superiors before walking down the aisle with the Vessel to offer James, Lucca, and Swinson the drink of our Superiors' blood. We walked towards each other, bowing at the altar and each saying the final verse of the ritual, reciting as that was all they were required to say.

"I will protect, I will not falter, all my life I serve the alter,

Protect the order and rise with rigour all."

James snatched the Vessel from me and once again, I wanted to punch him, but I contained myself. I ignored his smirk as he passed the Vessel back to me and hissed at me.

"Aren't you afraid your dad wants me more than you? He wishes I were his son. You are worthless."

I walked away with shaking hands and gave Lucca and Swinson their turn before heading back to the sanctuary. As soon as Swinson finished, the room burst into applause. I walked back to the front of the room and handed back the Vessel before taking my seat. I hoped the dreams and visions of the girl would end so I could fully embrace my inner Demon and stop dwelling on her.

After a few warnings about attacks on mortals and how they wouldn't be tolerated, we were dismissed. Most people hurried away from the enclave, but I waited as was expected of me. Lisa came over to talk to me after most people left and sat in Nick's vacated seat. She leaned in close and whispered, "I haven't seen you for ages." As she spoke, she ran her hand up my arm. Her touch made my skin crawl. I began turning towards her, ready to say something cutting, when I noticed my dad watching us from across the chamber. The look intrigued me. He looked almost happy to see us together, which surprised me. I turned to Lisa and forced my face into a smile.

"Sorry, babe. I had to study. My parents freaked out because I failed that stupid math test, but I'm free after this if you fancy doing something?"

"Yeah, that sounds lovely. Let me just go and say to my parents that I'm going away with you and we can meet outside when you're finished." She knew as candidate I had to stay for the entire meeting. As she walked away, sauntering in her skin-tight jeans and yellow blouse, my father came towards me. His light touch on my shoulder made me tense up, but I don't think he noticed.

"Go hang out with Lisa and Joe, but don't be late tonight..." I didn't need to be told twice and left quickly. I found Lisa waiting just outside the door and we headed in silence to the clearing.

CHAPTER 6

THE CONFESSION

We stopped in the woods and Lisa kissed me. I kissed her back, determined to try to feel something. As she moved her hands, she touched a spot on the bottom of my back through my jumper. I felt white-hot flames lick their way through me. I shuddered, which Lisa took it as an invitation to press harder and my eyes filled with tears.

I refused to let them fall and gently detangled myself from her. I held her hand and felt nothing, nothing at all. Her face was flushed, her blond hair tied up high in a hair clip with wisps falling over her face. Her blue eyes twinkled and she smiled as we walked towards the clearing.

She was beautiful, but my feelings were ambivalent at best. It was as though they had been erased. I felt as though I was a computer with a file missing and I had no idea at all how to retrieve it. We continued walking towards our friends. As we got closer to them, Joe met us halfway. We stood just away from the campfire in the centre of the clearing. All around, my friends laughed, drank, and had a great time.

I watched Joe as he moved towards us, brushing off any attempt at conversation. The firelight bounced around behind him, giving him an ethereal glow that made me laugh. He looked at me like I'd lost my mind. When he reached us, he looked at Lisa and smiled at her.

"Lisa, I need to borrow Nate for a bit, but would you be okay to keep my date company? She's new and I don't want her falling in with the wrong crowd." His eyes flickered to James and then back to me as I watched him.

My confusion must have been evident on my face because he gave me a small shake of his head as Lisa asked him, "Sure, who is it?"

My eyes roamed around the firelight, spotting her seconds before he answered. "Meghan. She's over by Lucca and James."

I growled as soon as Joe mentioned James, and Joe looked at me in surprise. He knew I didn't like James, but didn't know how deep my loathing of him went. Ever since I'd caught him with a dead mortal two months ago and reported him to my father, James had had it in for me. It had started small, but since that day, I'd caught him with another two mortals, both low on essence. He had vehemently denied it was he, claiming that someone was out to get him. He then told my father that it was I, and since then, relations with my parents had deteriorated to the point of no return. As soon as I was leader of my own assembly, I intended on only coming back for the Halloween feast and nothing else. James normally avoided these things, but if he was here, it was because he wanted to fuck with me.

Joe noticed my glare as I stared at James across the firelight and gave me a questioning look. I just shook my head at him, not ready to answer questions surrounded by so many people.

I glanced at Lisa as she turned and looked across the clearing towards Meghan. She looked stunning as she did, appearing as though she stood in the fire with flames flicking out behind her. She leaned forward to kiss me and I kissed her back, trying to feel something as I held her neck. I deepened the kiss, but all I felt was a detached disinterest. I let her go and turned to Joe, who whispered, "Was that really necessary? You're going to see her in like fifteen minutes and you almost screwed her in front of me. Cheers, mate. I feel really sick now."

I punched him in the arm, smiling at his words as we headed out of the clearing. With no need to explain where we were going, we both knew where to talk in private.

Joe and I worked our way through the woods, passing Mikey and his girl on a heavy kissing session. We averted our eyes as we noticed his wandering hands. Smirking at each other and laughing as we passed them. After a few minutes, we reached the cave we had discovered when scouting these woods years ago. We had wandered down a narrow path on the cliff face, wanting to see if we could get down to the rocks. As we climbed down, we noticed a little cave, no more than ten feet deep and ten feet in diameter. It was hidden both from above and the curved path, since it had overhanging rock. We had hung out there on a number of occasions over the years. When we matured enough to use our powers, we had placed some enchantments on the cave so only we could enter. If anyone else happened to pass by, it would just look like a piece of rock to them.

We went into the cave, stopping just inside the entrance before we turned, swiping our hands across the entrance muttering, *Noli Petubare,* which caused the roar of the wind and the ocean to quiet. Using our powers was technically not allowed, but my dad didn't mind if we wanted to experiment with them, as long as no mortals were seriously hurt when we did.

I watched Joe as he lit one of our candles, hidden underneath a pile of rocks. He pushed it into the lantern that sat directly beside it. It lit up the cave eerily without casting any light outside. I sat on a large rock next to Joe and he gazed at me, "What happened to you last night, man? I called your mobile and eventually Jenny answered and told me to fuck off."

I looked at my friend, the only person I had ever trusted with the truth about my parents, and smiled sadly. "I bet that pissed you off?"

"Yeah, it did. Stop avoiding and answer the question." I laughed at him, but also thought he was lucky. If anyone else spoke to me that way, I'd probably knock them out.

He smiled at the look on my face, but waved his arm for me to continue. I spoke, staring at the lantern, watching the flickering of the candle, sounding more robotic than Demon.

"I took a bad one last night." By bad one, we both knew I meant beating and for a moment, I stopped, as last night rushed back to me and my back stung with the reminder. My eyes wandered to the exit and I saw James prowling around, but our enchantment kept the cave hidden. Joe noticed him too and by the scowl on his face and the cracking of his knuckles, I could tell he wasn't happy. He stood and walked towards the entrance. I stood with him and I put my hand on his arm, stopping him.

"He's not worth it, mate. Just let it go. I'm gonna deal with him on my own."

"What? No, you're not. I've got your back. Remember?" He frowned down at me. "Why would you wanna deal with him on your own?"

I blurted out the truth, speaking without thinking, and annoyed myself.

"Because that asshole has it in for me and I wanna end him." The venom in my statement surprised us both. His eyebrows rose and he sat back down, and looked at me sceptically. "What is it, Joe?"

"Why are you becoming reckless? What do you have to prove? You're the candidate, for fuck sake? You're supposed to be beyond reproach."

My temperature rose and I paced the length of the cave before lunging at Joe. My face was inches from his as my Demon half took over and all my anger, helplessness, and pain from the last few days spilled out, "I am fucking human! I make mistakes! I might be a Demon but, for fuck sake, I can't be perfect all the time..." I panted with anger at him for calling me out on my attitude and I punched the wall behind his head. "My parents beat me so badly last night and left me in the dark for fucking hours. When my dad finally decided to heal me, he left me with a patch of the beating, just to remind me how powerless I am against them and how much they hate me. I can't fucking win! No matter what I do, it isn't ever good enough. And James is fucking sniffing around, trying to oust me while they're fucking with my mind..."

I let go of Joe and punched the wall again. I stalked around the cave, fighting to calm down. My body shook and shivered while my chest heaved. Joe stood where I had released him. He didn't speak for a few moments as I paced around and around, only massaging his neck before he muttered, "Feel better now?"

I glared over at him and hissed, "No... yeah... I don't fucking know." He laughed at me and I joined in as we sat heavily on the rocks again. He looked at me seriously for a few seconds before his face brightened.

"Wanna go back and get shitfaced?"

I started in surprise. I had expected him to ask what had happened, but I realised that he had heard these stories way too often over the years, especially over the last few months.

"Hell fucking yeah, I do!" We blew the candle out, covered it with the rocks, and walked towards the edge of the cave. Looking out, we could still see James on the path and I turned to Joe, "It would be so easy to push him off here and make it look like an accident."

"Ha-ha, yeah, it would, but knowing that fucker, he'd probably survive and grass you up."

"You're probably right... Joe, thanks."

"For what, mate?"

"Listening."

"Aww, are we turning into mortal girls now? Next, you wanna braid my hair and go see the Backstreet Boys?"

"Who the fuck are they?"

"A boy band my sister likes."

"Burnt Ashes are more my scene, but thanks."

"Eh, I haven't heard of them. Who the fuck are they?"

"They're a rock band. The lead singer has some set of pipes on him and the guitarist is shit hot. You should check them out on YouTube."

"Sometimes I wonder about you..."

I shook my head in despair. "Is the coast clear?"

"Yeah, I think so. We should probably head back quietly though, just in case that asshole's hovering about."

We didn't speak at all as we walked back. As we reached the clearing, James stepped out of the trees from behind us. He lunged at me, but I quickly sidestepped and he smashed headfirst into a tree. Both Joe and I walked into the firelight chortling, but he came from behind and grabbed me, throwing me roughly to the ground. He lifted his foot to kick me and I spun out of the way. I grabbed a hold of his foot and twisted until he landed on the ground. My body pounced on him as my Demon side took over, rage unleashing the power within me. I pushed my hand into his throat and held it there until he turned purple.

His face turned darker and darker as I hissed in his ear. My friends stood watching with a sort of detached interest. "That was a big mistake. In fact, that was a huge mistake. You just attacked me in front of all these witnesses. You had better listen to me, you sadistic fuck. I'm the Chief's son, not you. You will never replace me, and if you ever touch me again, I will fucking bury you. Got it?"

My eyes met his and he didn't move. I pressed slightly harder. He nodded his head with a look of hatred on his face. It made me smile and I stood, making sure I stepped on his hand as I walked away from him.

I saw Lisa across the clearing and sauntered over towards her, a spring in my step for the first time in ages. She held out a shot glass towards me, filled with golden liquid. As soon as I reached her, I knocked it back. I winced slightly as the tequila burned my insides. The alcohol warmed my stomach and I reached towards Lisa, pulling her into a passionate kiss. Still unable to feel anything, I turned away, leading her by the hand towards the music player. I put on some music, loud enough to drown my thoughts out and started back across the clearing.

Joe danced with Meghan, laughing at something she said. I glanced at them and smiled, but I was focused on one of the two portable tables set up in the shade of the trees. The one I headed for was covered in a black tablecloth with cups, punch bowls, and glasses. There was vodka, Jack, Morgan's, tequila, Aftershock, Jaeger, and other miscellaneous bottles.

I reached the table and pulled my hand out of Lisa's before pouring all different alcohols together into a large cup. Once the cup was full, I swallowed it in one gulp, wincing at the vileness of the taste as it hit the back of my throat. The alcohol burned, but also left my vision blurred at the edges. Lisa had walked away while I fixed my drink. She was probably in a huff because I had ignored her.

I loaded up with a variety of bottles from the table, and finding a plastic bag underneath, I stuck the bottles into the bag. At the next table, I found some snacks and a picnic blanket. I wandered around trying to find Lisa. I eventually found her speaking in a low voice to my sister. I walked over and both girls looked at me in alarm.

"Hey, sis," I muttered before turning to look at Lisa. "You fancy getting out of here?" She smiled shyly before nodding her head.

Grabbing her hand, I helped her to her feet. We slowly made our way through the woods, without discussing it, to the top of the cliffs. After a few moments of silence, she leaned over and whispered in my ear, "I want to, Nathan..."

The alcohol made me want her too and as I looked at her, I felt turned on by her for the first time in forever.

We reached the smaller clearing at the top of the cliffs where I spread out the blanket. She sat, pulling me down with her, and stared at me through lustful eyes. I started kissing her and the girl popped into my head again. Instead of making out with Lisa, I turned her in my mind into that girl and my body responded. My heart pounded and my blood raced around my veins.

I ran my hand across her ribs, feeling her breathing stutter as my hand trailed downwards and curled around her waist. I kissed down her neck and she pulled my jumper away from my back while whispering in my ear, "I've missed you, missed us." As she pulled, the fabric tore away the healing skin and her touch burned me like a white-hot poker to my back. Her voice broke the spell and I sat up on my heels, panting as though I had just run a marathon. *What am I doing? Why do I have to replace her in my mind to be attracted to her? What is going on with me? How am I okay with this?* I pulled further away and stared intently at her. She was pretty in the moonlight, but she wasn't who I wanted and I couldn't use her. I pulled her up with me and wrapped my arms around her waist, my front to her back.

I opened a bottle of cider for each of us and we sat, lost in our own thoughts for a while. My thoughts were consumed by the girl with the brown hair and hazel eyes. I saw her everywhere, but I realised I held onto her and that I had to let go. Otherwise, I would ruin my relationship with Lisa.

After that thought, I watched the moon rise higher in the sky. The waves rushed in over and over, until eventually we had consumed all the drinks and it was time to head back. I stood, leaned my hand down to help Lisa, and as she put her hand in mine, a flicker of what I had felt for her overwhelmed me.

I yanked her closer and put my hand underneath her hair, stroking her face with my other hand. I leaned over hesitantly and placed my lips on hers.

I tugged on her bottom lip with my teeth, my hands slipping down the side of her breasts and she gasped, pulling me in closer. I pushed her over to a large tree, a few feet behind us. We moved without breaking apart as we both breathed heavily. We kissed with a passion I hadn't felt in weeks.

I lifted her against the tree so she perched slightly higher over me and gripped the hem of her top, twisting it in my fingers. I was just pulling it up when a throat clearing made us both jump apart as though we had been scalded. My brother stood there, his lips turned down although it looked like he was fighting a smirk. He held a lantern aloft and laughed as he spoke. "If you two have finished, I need to borrow my brother, Lisa. Nate, it's twenty minutes till curfew. I thought I'd better find you."

The thought of facing my father's anger again made me jump. I gave Lisa a quick kiss before jogging over to my brother. Lisa watched us walk away with a frown, but I didn't bother looking back. Demon girls got pissed if you looked back. They were as strong as males and if we tried to tell them any different, they'd kick our asses. After a few minutes of silence, Nick looked at me and whispered, "Fifteen minutes, bro; we better hurry."

He started to run, faster than I could keep up. We ran through the woods in the pitch black with the only light coming from the swinging lantern Nick held. I knew where I was going, but that didn't stop me from flying over a tree root. I shot up, running until my back felt like it would break, and my lungs felt as though they were being crushed. As we reached the driveway, Nick turned around. "Take a mint. You're swaying around and if Dad catches you drinking, he'll undo the enchantment, and you'll really be in for it then."

I snorted at him, but took one from him as we continued to walk into the silent house. The house was deathly quiet, which was a bad sign. We looked around and walked towards the stairs when the office door slid open, throwing a little light into the dark hallway.

"Nathan, come in here please," my father's voice drifted into the hallway, causing Nick to throw me a worried glance. I began towards his office as my palms sweat. I felt like it was the walk to the gallows. My heart pounded with every step I took. My hands shook as I wiped them onto my jeans. The flashbacks started as I reached the door handle and I stumbled as I remembered being beaten to a pulp on my last visit to my father's office. I ended up in the hospital with a fractured wrist. He hit me so hard I bounced off his desk and landed awkwardly. I grasped the door handle to keep myself steady, and took a slow shaky breath before I went through the door.

CHAPTER 7
SURPRISES

The instant I took my first step inside the door, a bag went over my head and I groaned as I was punched hard in the stomach. My breath hissed out in a gasp and I was dragged backwards by my arms. I struggled, but my hands were bound and my heart raced. The last time they tied my hands like this was when I was whipped and I almost whimpered, only just managing to stop the sound by swallowing it back down. The only sound was my heart as the blood rushed around my ears and the light breathing of the people at either side of me.

Once we were outside, I was dragged down the stairs, causing my heart to leap into my throat. Outside meant I was being taken to the barn; that meant the punishment was too severe and too bloody for inside the house. The sounds reverberated in my head, my screams of agony from the last time we were in the barn got louder and louder until I almost screamed, dragging my heals to stop them from taking me in there.

Once I heard the doors creaking open, my heart rate sped up again and my breath came in short sharp gasps. My eyes teared, but before we got more than three feet into the barn, the arm ties were cut and the cover over my head was removed.

As the cover lifted, the room shouted surprise and I stumbled, blinking in the light. Most of my friends were there surrounded by my family. I realised that I'd completely forgotten about the Inauguration party. *What kind of idiot forgets their Inauguration party? Seriously? I am a complete moron.*

I looked around the room and smiled at everyone, relief flooding through me. I turned to my brother and glared at him when he sauntered up beside us. I punched him on the shoulder, laughing as I did, the residual fear making me giddy, "You asshole! You could've at least warned me."

"No chance. I woulda been murdered if I tried."

"That was really fucking mean, dude."

"Stop being such a fucking toddler. I can't believe you forgot Inauguration. Anyway, you remember my party. They tied me to the fucking tree. I thought I was done for and you didn't say anything to me either, fuckface!"

I stood there with Nick and watched our parents greet our guests as we joked around. I glanced around the room, saw a stunningly attractive blonde walk up to my brother, and snake her arms around his waist before kissing him fully on the mouth.

"I think I just threw up a little bit," I muttered before turning to walk away.

"Ha, now at least you know how I felt watching you and Lisa's little display tonight."

I turned away, wondering what attracted all these stunning girls to my brother. Every single time he came back from his flat near his uni, he had another stunner on his arm. First, it was leggy Denise, then Alexandra, and now this girl. Ever since he had split with Leanne in May, he was like a walking, talking babe magnet.

I wandered through the crowd, talking to my cousins, uncles, aunts, and friends. I spotted Joe and Meghan, and started to make my way over to them. Before I had even taken a few steps, a hand grasped my arm. I looked around and to my left, there were a number of people, but James stood on my right, shifting nervously from foot to foot as he looked around the room. I looked down at his arm, thinking of it burning and he let go with a yelp. Good, I had hurt him.

"This looks like you touching me again. Choose a spot, James, cause I'm gonna fucking bury you."

"Mate, can we talk?"

I drew my fist back to punch him, more than angry with him. I felt murderous, especially over him calling me mate and touching me after my warning. Just as I was about to let my fist fly, not one, not two, but three people grabbed my arm from behind, and two people grabbed him. I allowed them to pull me outside, but I still strained to get to him. Ramped up, I could feel my face hardening as the power and strength that only came from my Demon side rose to the surface.

Nick slammed into me and I almost caught him with my clawed hands. He ducked and punched me hard in the stomach. I retaliated and punched him hard in the gut. He flew away from me, his brown eyes swimming as he coughed, trying to catch his breath. Joe slammed into me, pushing me behind the barn.

"Nate... Nate, stop. Look at me... it's Joe... you don't wanna hulk out here... calm down." He looked at me, and I still felt the murderous rage pulsing through me as Joe spoke again. "Nate, for fuck sake, calm down."

I looked at him through black pits, but felt myself swimming back to the surface. I could see Nick lying where he landed as Joe talked me down from the rage that consumed me. *Where had that come from? I couldn't believe I had almost gone for someone. This has to have something to do with James. What the fuck has he done? He almost exposed us.*

"Fuck, fuck, fuck," I shouted, turning away from Joe and walking towards the woods. I needed to hit something, preferably that asshole's smug face repeatedly.

I ran towards the trees, but hadn't gone far when two hooded figures stepped out from the trees. The sight of them stopped me cold. I studied them intently. As I figured out what they were, I felt stunned that they had come here. After a few seconds of us staring at each other, one of them finally spoke and their voice gave me chills. "We must speak with the Chief. Candidate, get him now!"

I didn't move straight away. I was stunned by their appearance, and still felt sluggish because of the rage and the alcohol in my system. After another moment of standing there, I felt like I was drowning. Water filled my lungs and my body dropped like a stone. My mouth wouldn't open and I couldn't breathe in. Spots popped in my vision and her face swam into my mind again.

After a second, they both moved closer to me, their soulless black eyes trained on my face.

"Enough, Bartholomew. We have business to attend to and killing the Transference candidate would only expedite death for us. We are greatly outnumbered and do not want to be murdered like our brother. Stop it now."

As he spoke, his sightless eyes turned towards me and his skin glowed bright in the moonlight, pale white and colder than ice. Almost at once, as I was released, I threw myself onto my stomach. I coughed out what felt like water, but it was actually a sticky blackness. It burned like acid on the way up, making me retch and throw up violently. They moved beyond me and continued their way across the grass towards my friends and family. I managed to sit up even though my head swam and I couldn't clear it by shaking. I placed my hands on my head and my vision became less cloudy with each passing second, although my throat felt as though someone had lit a match inside it.

These creatures looked like Black-Eyed Beings. They were pale, almost iridescent, as they crossed the yard and took on various colours as they moved. Beings didn't normally leave their caves so for them to turn up, especially when they had been fighting with our family for many generations, meant something serious was afoot. They were our enemies and this visit would have serious repercussions. I was sure of it.

The night was clear and the moon was high in the sky, meaning I was able to see my brother and friends as they approached. Each face looked wary and Joe glanced between them, Nick, and me. Nick stepped towards them, speaking to them politely and with respect, "Marc and Bartholomew, what a surprise! How can we help you gentlemen?"

I wondered how he knew their names as I tried to get up.

"Nicholas, fetch your father at once. We have urgent business to discuss with him and we cannot do it in the open."

Nick looked at me as I stumbled my way over to them. I could still see spots in my vision and felt very weak from the venom that had filled me when they arrived.

"Hurry," Marc called to Nick. Nick scuttled off and Marc turned to look at Bartholomew, staring at him while I stumbled and tripped. My hands slammed down and I pushed myself back up, continuing across the garden towards them.

Just as I reached Joe, I stumbled and he righted me. Lisa walked out of the barn and moved beside me. She slipped her hands around my waist. Leaning into her was the best choice I could make since my legs felt like jelly and could barely hold me up. I didn't want to show any weakness to these creatures, especially after what had already happened to me.

I kissed her head, grateful to her for helping me, and caught Joe's eyes. He looked wary and scared and I was sure he saw the same, looking right back at him from my eyes. I worried that they were here because something bad had happened and for every second we stood in the yard, my feelings of foreboding increased. Seconds later, though it felt like hours, my father arrived.

"Marc, Bartholomew, what a surprise. To what do we owe this visit?" He sounded cordial, though I could hear the tension and anger in his voice. One glance at Nick told me he did as well.

"Can we take this inside?" Marc asked, sounding curt and irritated.

"Of course!" My mother's voice came from behind me. "Where are your manners, Lewis? Follow me."

CHAPTER 8
REPERCUSSIONS

As they walked towards the house, my uncle followed them from the door of the barn. He was closely followed by Greg and two other council members.

"What the fuck was that about?" I croaked out. Nick answered before anyone else could.

"Yeah, I don't get what's going on. First Rambo here hulks out and tries to attack everyone and then they arrive almost immediately after."

I turned to my brother and opened my mouth to apologise, but he shook his head at me. Joe spoke up in the uncomfortable silence that followed.

"That wasn't Nate, Nick. It was James; he touched Nate's arm and after a few words, I saw Nate shimmer. That's when I knew I had to get him outside. Although most in the barn are Demons, there are a few enchanted mortals and I didn't want him exposing us."

Fuck, I nearly exposed us, the sight of me demoning out would have broken through any enchantments placed on the fucking mortals and I would have been a dead man.

My head swam as my body reeled from the realisation that I could have exposed my world and had some of their playthings killed for no reason.

"Is that true?" my brother's voice broke through the fog and as I nodded, he walked towards me and pulled my arm into his hand. Everyone stared at my arm, including me, noticing as we did that there was a vibrant red handprint there. "Nate, your phone? Where is it?" I reached into my pocket and pulled out my phone. Nick snatched it, who then took a photo and studied it in complete silence. We watched him until he turned and showed the phone to everyone. "Fuck, Nate, that asshole doped you with Woodrose. No wonder you freaked. No wonder you hulked out. Our skin reacts to Woodrose and enough of it in the bloodstream makes us perceive everyone as a threat..."

He broke off as the house door opened behind us and our mother called to us.

"Nathan, Nicholas, come in here now." We turned at the same time and walked towards the stairs. My mother wasn't paying any attention to Nick; she was too busy drawing daggers at my head.

While we walked, Nick leaned down, "Don't say anything about the handprint or the evidence yet. Let's hear what they say before you mention it."

"Why?" is all I said as we walked into the house.

He was quiet as we continued along the hallway, but before we followed my mother towards the dining room, he muttered, "Don't worry, little bro. I have a plan." With that, he smiled at me from the corner of his mouth before stepping ahead of me into the room.

I moved to follow him when my mother smacked me full force on the back, right on the spot my father hadn't healed and my eyes streamed. I wiped them on my sleeve and followed her, swallowing the pain and feeling my sense of foreboding increase with every step I took into the dining room.

The further into the room I trudged, the more serious the situation seemed. All of the Superiors stood in a closed circle. Nick, Jack, and my mother stood off to the side nearer the window and the dining table, which had been pushed against the far wall. The Black-Eyed Beings stood off to the side and as I glanced around, my brother looked at me in dismay. *Shit, this is going to be bad. This is going to be very, very bad.*

As one, all eyes turned to me — the council members, my mother, my brother, and the visitors. My father looked at me, his face more Demon than human in his anger, "Nathan, go sit in the kitchen. Now!"

I looked around them all, stunned. My brother's forehead wrinkled with worry as he ran his fingers through his hair. I left the room, passing my uncle who, when I made eye contact, just shook his head at me. My uncle was supposed to be my friend. We had become close when he lived with us, though now he looked at me as though I was a stranger.

As I closed the door, I caught a glimpse of the Ceremonial Blade that we had used in the Inauguration ceremony. It lay on the serving table beside the door covered in some black liquid.

What is that doing here? The knife was usually locked up in our vault, under the church, and for it to be here was very significant. I just couldn't figure out quite what the significance was for me, and then I remembered. As the candidate for this term's Inauguration, it was my responsibility to put the knife and chalice away. *Oh fuck!* I'd forgotten. *Oh fuck, fuck, major fuck.* Not putting that knife away securely meant a severe punishment. My palms started sweating and I looked around the kitchen for an escape. My eyes landed on the back door, but I knew I couldn't do it. I was a Demon and we took punishments as a way to make us stronger.

I couldn't shift the fear of what would happen as I gazed down at my hands. They were shaking. I moved to the breakfast bar in the kitchen and slumped down onto a chair. My eyes darted around the room and my whole body shook in dread. I pushed my hands under my legs and sat on them, which helped a little. It didn't help calm my mind as I considered all the possibilities of what would happen to me. I had to try to man up and stop acting like such a pussy.

A door opened, which made me jump, and I quickly looked towards the kitchen door, but it was actually the back door. Jenny walked in, looked at me, and walked right past me without saying a word. Sometimes my family really made me feel like a complete outsider, unwanted and unwelcome in their house. Lisa followed her over the threshold and stopped when she saw me sitting at the breakfast bar alone.

As soon as Lisa's eyes met mine, she walked over to me and touched my shoulder. Jenny looked at us both, shook her head, and turned away. "I'm away upstairs. Lisa; come up when you're done." She let the door swing shut behind her.

Even though I was confused over my feelings for Lisa, I wrapped my arms tightly around her waist and put my head against her stomach. I shuddered and she stroked my head softly, running her fingers through my hair.

"Nathan, what's wrong?" Her tone was bewildered, but I just shook my head against her stomach and closed my eyes. I stayed like that for a few moments before reaching up and twisting my hand behind her neck as I drew her in to kiss me. I took comfort from the kiss and didn't hear my father enter the room.

"Lisa, leave now!" my father's voice bellowed across the kitchen. The sound of his voice made me jump as though I had been electrocuted. "Nathan, come with me." His tone was glacial.

Lisa scuttled out of the kitchen with a respectful, "Yes, sir." As soon as she was gone, my fear increased and I stood on shaking legs. I followed Lisa and my father out of the kitchen. I moved straight and tall into the dining room, although I was unsure what I was walking into.

"Sit." My father pointed to a chair in the middle of the room and I went towards it, my eyes focused the entire walk on the chair. The chair was one of our usual dining chairs, though as soon as I sat, I felt as though I was completely glued to the seat. "Nathan Daniel Stevenson, you have been called here as this year's Transference candidate. You will be asked a series of questions and for every lie you tell, you will be cut with the Ceremonial Blade, which has been dipped in hogweed solution. Do you understand?" I tried to nod, even though I couldn't move my head. I took a breath, opened my mouth, and spoke in a high, clear voice, which surprised me.

"Yes, sir." *They plan to burn me. Hogweed is a burning plant used for interrogating adversaries.*

"Okay, we begin. Who is the Transference candidate?"

"I am, sir." I was surprised that I sounded so calm when my insides jumped around like a car in a hurricane.

"And what, as candidate, are your responsibilities?"

"To uphold Demon values, to protect our sacrifice, and to procreate with at least two separate desirables!" I sounded off, answering quickly as my eyes darted around.

"Are those all the values or all you can think of?"

"All the values?" I asked, wondering why my father treated me like a criminal and why the visitors watched me with hunger in their eyes. My eyes moved around the room, thinking about the values when my father dragged the blade across my arm. The cut itself wasn't deep, but the pain was intense and almost instantaneous. It felt as though he had poured acid on my skin. I glanced down at my arm and I could see bubbles forming just under the skin that had turned a bright pink colour.

While I sat there panting, my father backed away and continued, "Are there perhaps any things you forgot to do, in your excitement as candidate?" I stared at him as I struggled to understand what he was talking about. His eyes widened and his nostrils flared as I watched him. Then it hit me — the knife and how it was my responsibility to put it safely away.

"Yes, I did. I forgot to put away the Ceremonial Blade."

"Did you know it was your responsibility?"

"Yes," I whispered in a small voice.

"Why did you forget?"

"I'm not sure!" Why did I forget? I knew the penalty if the knife were to go missing so what had caused me to forget to put the knife in the vault? I wasn't sure at all and I didn't want to lie so I said nothing else. My father pressed the knife hard into my other arm, on top of where the handprint had been. The skin split like paper and the cut was deeper than he expected it to be, judging from the shocked look in his eyes as he glanced up at me.

My eyes watered, as the burning took hold and I felt as though I would be sick with the flames racing through me. I was only able to see my father vaguely; he stood at the edge of my field of vision. I didn't notice a stirring at the back of the room, but my lungs filled again. I choked, unable to move and unable to breathe.

"Enough, Bartholomew!" A terse voice sounded from the back of the room, but I was unable to verify to whom it belonged. My eyes clouded over and I blacked out into the darkness. I welcomed the darkness and its ability to rid me of the ache of the knife cuts and the pain in my back.

After a few minutes, or hours, I came to, and found myself still sitting in the chair, but with my throat now on fire as well. My father continued as though there had been no interruption. "Nathan, you were about to tell us what happened. Please continue." I urged myself to make something up, a voice in my head all but shouted at me. I tried to shake my head to clear my thoughts, but I still couldn't move.

"I was excited to see my friends," I whispered, my voice cracking and throat burning as I told the first thing that came into my head. My father started to cut me again and I felt my skin pull away. The fire that tore through the cut seared down to my soul, my very essence, but I couldn't free myself from it. My breath came in gasps and I saw my brother step towards my father. He whispered something to our father and stepped back out of the circle.

"Are you sure?" my father asked. All I could hear was fury in his voice and it made the hairs on my arms rise up. I wasn't sure if he was speaking to Nick, or me but I decided to answer anyway because I didn't want to be cut or burnt again.

"Yes, sir, well my friends and my girlfriend." My answer seemed to have satisfied him because he looked at me thoughtfully.

"Where did you go after the ceremony?"

"To the clearing?" I answered, watching in fear as my father again walked towards me. He swiped the blade across my skin on my left arm and the skin ripped like paper and sizzled. The sound of my skin fizzling made me gag. I managed not to throw up even though my eyes watered and lips trembled.

"Did you stay in the clearing?" He asked, interest replacing fury.

"No, I went to a smaller one with Lisa later in the evening." He didn't seem satisfied with my answer and came towards me again. I cried out this time as the burning sensation overtook my mind. I couldn't think beyond the scorching heat roaring through my arm. It felt as though it was being held over an open flame, as though someone ran a candle up and down my arm while I was frozen, unable to move. Tears clouded my vision and I blinked them back, swallowing hard as he asked his next question.

"Did you go anywhere else?"

Wondering why it was relevant, I answered slowly, "Yeah, I went for a walk with Joe."

"Where did you go?"

"We wandered to the cliff face and around the woods."

"Did you see anyone there?"

"Yes, we saw James, but didn't stop to speak to him."

"Why not?"

"I don't like James much!" I answered honestly, wondering why on Earth all this was relevant. I saw Greg moving towards my father and the venom in his expression as he looked at me was surprising. As a Superior, Greg should have looked ambivalent or detached, but he looked at me in plain hatred. I tried to think about what I could possibly have done to offend him to the point of hatred. I couldn't think of anything other than the fact I was a week older than James, meaning I was the official candidate and he was not. Suddenly my father made an announcement.

"We shall take a break and come back to this in twenty minutes. Nick, fetch James."

They all left one by one until only my uncle remained. I guessed he watched me, though I couldn't see him clearly as he still stood off to the side.

"Nate, what the fuck happened? Your father has been telling me some very disturbing facts about you?"

"Like what?" I asked, wondering why he wasn't walking to where I could see him.

"About how you're disrespecting them, about you consuming mortals, and fucking around with another Demon girl behind your girlfriend's back. How about you disappearing with your friend and then reappearing with no one knowing where you went? What the fuck is going on, Nathan?"

How do they know about Amy? I haven't told anyone about that so how the fuck does my father know? Oh my God, are they going to torture Joe? Would he tell them about the cave? Fuck.

As these thoughts ran through my head, my uncle stepped into my line of sight, his face looking years older as he stared at me. I didn't answer his question. I didn't have good enough reasons for my recent behaviour. I decided to ask him a question to deflect his thoughts from me and onto why I was here, being tortured.

"What's this about, Jack? I don't get why I'm here."

"I can't tell you; it's forbidden, though I'm sure you'll find out soon enough." As he said that, he stepped away and went back to wherever he stood before he moved.

"Why can't you tell me? What's going on? Come on, Jack. Please?" I begged him. I needed someone to be on my side and Jack usually was. He maintained a stony silence for the rest of the time we were in the room alone, not moving or answering my pleas for information.

The room felt oppressive and the silence pressed down on me like a tonne weight. Eventually, after a few more minutes of sitting in silence, my father and his fellow council members returned, each staring at me as they entered the room. They were followed by the visitors. The last in were my mother and Nick, who held a beaten and bloody Joe.

One of Joe's eyes was closed and he grimaced in pain with blood dripping from his mouth as they dragged him into the room. My father spoke without looking at me, "It has been decided that Joseph will be questioned next, followed by James. In this way, we shall be able to determine whether Nathan has been telling the truth and we should be able to find out who the murderer is and deal with them accordingly." The word murderer stood out. *What murderer? Who had been murdered?* He turned to me, "Nathan, you are released at present. You must remain as some thirst for Demon blood. To kill you would send a clear message about what happened earlier tonight."

He spoke and I was finally able to move, but I stayed slumped in the chair. I felt as though I had no energy whatsoever. After a few moments, I stood and stumbled towards my mother, Nick, and Jack. I reached them, pulled out a chair, and fell into it as the process started all over again with Joe. He was cut a few times as well, but told the same story as I did, only omitting the cave. Eventually he was let go, although he had to stay to find out what his verdict would be.

James, however, appeared to be the one responsible. He confessed to seeing the knife being taken and looking for Joe and me in the woods. Watching him being questioned was so interesting that I almost forgot how exhausted and in pain I was.

"Why did you follow Joe and Nathan?"

"Sir, I was worried that Swinson was going after them. You see when I saw him take the knife, he muttered under his breath about taking out all those in his way to becoming candidate. He spoke especially of hurting Nathan."

At this point Joe and exchanged a sceptical glance and shook our heads. "I was worried he would go after Nathan so I followed them."

"Why then did you attack Nathan in the clearing upon their return?" My father looked at him without the loathing he often wore when he looked at me.

"I am not proud of it, sir, but he was goading me and I snapped."

"Goading you in what way?"

"Laughing because I wouldn't be candidate and cursing at me..." he broke off and began crying. Upon looking around, I could see I was not the only one who found this performance disgraceful.

"So that gave you cause to attack my son?" Now my father was angry, I could tell from his tone and the look on his face.

"No, sir. It did not, but I lost it."

"What happened next?"

"I left the clearing upon Nathan's order and wandered through the woods, heading home. This was when I stumbled upon Swinson and the dead Black-Eyed Being. He stood with the Ceremonial Blade in his hands, smiling as he stabbed the creature over and over again, even though it was clearly dead."

While he spoke, I looked around the room and saw uneasy faces staring at him. Swinson killing one of these creatures was punishable by death. James knowing about it and not reporting it was almost as bad. He could be banished or worse. I hoped for worse for him, but I had to stop dreaming about killing James as my father asked, "What did you do then?"

"I came here intending to ask Nathan for advice, though when I touched him, he almost lost it, starting to turn into a Demon in the barn."

My father turned and glared at me until I looked away, colour staining my cheeks as I remembered going for Nick. "Nathan, is that true?"

"Yes, sir, but..."

"There will be time for you to explain your reasoning for almost transforming in a party with mortals present later. For now, I must continue. We have much to get through." He turned his back on me and my insides burned with shame at the fact that I had almost exposed us.

"James, what happened next?"

"Nathan took off running and from what I could see; he ran into the Beings as they arrived on the property."

CHAPTER 9
THE VERDICTS

"Fine, you are free to go. The three of you, Nathan, Joseph, and James, will all wait in the kitchen while we discuss the evidence presented to us here tonight. We shall return with our verdicts shortly."

We sat around the breakfast bar in the kitchen. Joe sat beside me, blood still dripping from his lip, but he ignored it completely. Across from us sat James, smirking.

"You had something to do with this," I glared at him, unable to believe that this was how my Inauguration party would end. Joe put his hand on my shoulder, holding me in place while James smirked at me.

"If I did, I'm not likely to tell you, am I?"

Just as I was about to move, the kitchen door opened and my brother stepped in, "Joe, come with me please." I clapped Joe on the shoulder as he stood, the only way I could thank him for his loyalty in omitting the cave and to wish him luck in what he would face. Demons were not well known for their leniency.

I started to ask what was going on, but stopped at the look Nick gave me. He shook his head and walked out, holding the door for Joe. Joe leaned over me before he left, throwing a glare at James before whispering in my ear. "Don't react to him. We'll find a way to get rid of him one way or another. Just don't lose your shit. Try to ignore him." He straightened up before heading out into the dining room where his fate would be decided.

I ignored James completely and sat in stony silence, thinking about how I wanted to cut him open and rip out his insides. I decided that these thoughts made me angrier so I focused on the thought of the girl again and it calmed me down. I put my head in my hands on the breakfast bar as I pictured her face, brown hair floating around in the breeze, full lips smiling at me, and her hazel eyes beguiling me as I moved closer to her. My head dropped off my arms and I managed to catch myself before I fell asleep.

I looked anywhere but at James. I noticed that the night sky outside the window began to lighten, making me realise it was in the early hours of Sunday morning. I was exhausted and hoped it would be over soon. I just wanted to go to bed.

Moments later, the kitchen door opened and Greg, James' dad, walked in. He didn't even look at me, but walked straight over to his son, whispering urgently in his ear. I watched as they both stood together to leave the kitchen. I said nothing, although I ached to open my mouth. Somehow, I managed to keep it closed. Greg turned around and glared at me. I didn't react. Exhaustion had stolen my fire and I just watched with a bored expression as they left. At the last second, he seemed to change his mind; he stormed over to me and punched me in the mouth, sending me flying backwards into the range.

He scuttled over towards the door and as the door shut, I saw James laughing as he stepped into the dining room. Feeling enraged, I jumped to my feet and paced around the room, but the events of the previous few days crept up on me. After a few minutes, I sagged back down onto my chair.

I was worried, more worried than I would have admitted to anyone. I had failed in one of my key responsibilities. Knowing I had let my father down weighed heavily on me and I felt almost suffocated by guilt. I shook my head again knowing that I had to be strong. I had to become more like my father and stop letting myself get carried away by emotions. Emotions were human and they didn't belong in the Demon world or help solve anything.

I started to drift off so I stood again and went over to the coffee machine to make myself a strong cup. I needed one to stay awake and to warm me up. I felt ice cold inside. After I made the coffee, I sat staring at myself in the mirrored cabinet. My brown hair was messy, curls drifting down to my neck, my green eyes looked dimmer than usual and bags sat under my eyes that hadn't been there a few days ago. I took a sip of my coffee and winced. The tenderness in my throat caused it to ache.

"If you have finished admiring yourself in the mirror, they've reached a verdict about you," Nick called from the doorway. He watched as I drained my coffee and placed the cup in the dishwasher. "Whenever you're ready. Take your time, Nate. I'm in no rush."

I looked at him as I made my way over, but he didn't smile at me, or give me any indication of what I was in for. When I entered the room, there was a pool of blood on the floor and I looked around in shock, backing away. Nick pushed me slightly. I glared at him as I stumbled forward.

"Sit down, Nathan!" my father's voice came authoritatively from the doorway. I obeyed. I was able to move in the chair and upon sweeping the room, I noticed that James, his father, and Joe were all missing. I didn't comment on that; it didn't seem like the appropriate time.

"Nathan, you are here because you did not obey the commands of your Superiors. By not putting away the Ceremonial Blade, you may have started another war with the Beings who were here earlier. This has been averted, but punishments must be delivered. As you were responsible for the knife, you are also responsible for the killing of a Being. As such, I sentence you to forty lashes, to take place over the next two days. May you learn your lesson and follow all future responsibilities to the letter," he broke off and I gasped. He looked at me through cold eyes as I struggled to take in what he was saying. "All in favour, stand now?"

I stared at the ground for a beat before I dragged my eyes up and scanned the room, distracted by a ringing sound in my ears. I saw my mother standing, my brother standing, my uncle sitting, and my sister standing. I hadn't even noticed that Jenny was at the meeting, but she wouldn't look at me. I moved my eyes reluctantly on, not wanting to move. I was sure most of the council members would be standing. I was right and my heart hammered loudly in my ears.

I swallowed convulsively and met my father's furious glare. He continued to glare at me as he said severely, "Motion passed. Nicholas, Jennifer, take your brother to the barn and tie him to the tree. I will be there momentarily."

They walked me across in complete silence, tied me up, and left me there. I sagged against the ropes, breathing hard and wondering how long it would be until I died. *Perhaps if I am dead, I won't be such a failure. Maybe this will kill me and put me out of my misery.*

I don't know how long I stood there listening to the sway of the branches of the oak tree. The wind whistled through the cracks in the barn, causing the door to creak open and closed. The sounds of the door distracted me enough that I didn't hear their footsteps. The only warning I got before being hit was my mother cutting my jumper and top away from my back so the whip would hit me on the bare skin.

The whip whistled through the air, cracking loudly on my back and around my ribs. The whip hit me and I groaned in pain as the flames licked over me. There was no respite. The hits came in quick succession and I screamed loudly on the third one. The pain was unbearable and I blacked out a few times through the whipping. My father pulled me back so I would feel every single hit of the whip. The fourth hit was worse and after the tenth hit, I sagged against the ropes. When the hits finally stopped, I vomited all over my legs and shoes. I retched until my stomach was empty, though each time felt like I was burned.

Everyone who had gathered to watch my whipping walked out after the tenth hit and I shivered, feeling both hot and cold at the same time. While I slumped against the ropes, her sweet face came unbidden into my mind and I pictured her smiling at me. Her eyes lit up as she looked at me, and my heart stuttered in response. She became my lifeline, my candle in the darkness. She was the only light I could see and I held onto her with everything I had as the pain rolled over me constantly.

Later in the afternoon found me still in the same position. I hadn't had any more whippings, though I knew one must be coming, I hadn't been allowed to move so I was a mess, covered in blood, sweat, and other body fluids. My arms burned and ached as though someone had tied weights to them.

Almost as soon as the sun moved across the afternoon sky, they were all back. I could see Jenny and Nick standing at the door, watching as I was lashed again, another ten. I didn't think I had much skin left, but after this whipping, my father healed the skin and left the pain. He fixed only what could be seen, though he made sure that I could still feel every single lesion.

This happened again the next time, although the final time, he didn't heal me. Instead, he left me with the cuts. I screamed in agony and tears streamed down my face. I counted each hit of the whip, blacking out repeatedly. Finally, it was over and the ropes binding me were cut. I collapsed in a heap on the floor. My family all walked out and left me. I was weak, weaker than ever and I couldn't stand, or walk. I couldn't even use my arms.

I could barely remember who I was. The pain was all-consuming, wiping out everything as it scorched through me and I retched again and again. Her face swam in my vision again. I could barely focus on it as every fibre of my being focused on how to survive this pain. My heart hammered loudly in my ears and I finally felt my vision cloud over with blackness as I pictured her lips caressing my own. Darkness took me and I stayed slumped, curled in a ball at the bottom of the tree before finally drifting into unconsciousness.

I woke after what felt like no time at all, with bread and water set next to me, along with a note.

Nathan, there is medicine in the water which will heal your wounds. You must go to school tomorrow, though today you may have one sick day. I do not expect you to have anymore and we shall discuss how to move forward tonight when I am home from work.

Dad.

I gulped the water down, feeling relieved that I would feel better after it. I sagged against the tree as the inferno on my back dulled to a mild ache and ate the bread slowly as my body responded to the medicine.

After a few more minutes, I got up, went into the house, and went for a shower before collapsing in a heap on my bed. I slept fitfully for a while, but didn't feel rested. I dreamed of her again. We walked through the woods, laughing. Her laugh, so light and carefree, took root in my soul. I felt lighter in my dream, happier, and content with her. I didn't ever want to wake up. The sound of a door slamming downstairs pulled me from my dream and I rolled over, trying without success to get back to sleep.

I stayed in my room most of the day, sleeping, studying, and eating so I could avoid Nick, who was still at home, and my mum, who glared at me every single time I passed her. Eventually, after a few hours of solace, Nick came into my room to fetch me. He didn't look at me and didn't acknowledge that I was his brother, or that I was scared.

"Dad wants to speak to you in his study." He looked over my head as he spoke. He didn't bother to wait for me and I was glad. Although I had resolved to become more Demon, I was still a scared sixteen-year-old.

I went into the bathroom and splashed cold water on my face before I looked at the mirror. My reflection shocked me. My eyes were a dark jade today, my teeth chewing on my lip and bags under my eyes made me look exhausted. As I stared at my reflection, the girl swam in my vision again, but I shook it off. I needed a clear head to face my father and deal with the consequences of my irresponsibility.

Forcing myself to walk out of my room towards the stairs took more courage than I had ever needed before. I knew that there would be some very serious repercussions for my actions. Had I just locked the knife up, the last three days wouldn't have happened; we would have had a fun party and life would have resumed a normal pace on Sunday instead of the punishments that had been administered. I walked further towards the stairs, glancing across at the guest bedroom that had been empty since Nick went to university.

As I walked, I could feel my skin prickling on my neck and my breathing quicken. I had to stop and scrub my face with my hands to rid myself of these feelings. I couldn't show any signs of weakness or I would be right back in the barn.

When I reached the bottom of the stairs, I noticed the time on the clock;

it read 13:04. My dad didn't usually get in from the hospital until little after six every night. The fact that he was home this early was as surprising as it was scary. My father never left early, ever. I continued making my way towards his office, though I stopped at the threshold. The look on my father's face froze me mid-step. This wasn't over yet.

"Ah, Nathan, come in and sit down. Now, we have to talk about your actions on Saturday. I have had to leave work to come back and try to clean up your mess. Hurry up and sit down, boy."

I sat and couldn't stop myself from shaking as I looked at my father, waiting with trepidation to hear his next words. As he spoke, some of the tension inside me unravelled, but not enough for me to relax completely.

"As you know, James has accused Swinson of the murder of another immortal creature and this carries the severest of consequences. I wanted to hear your take on this. You have attended school with both boys and I believe you are friends with Swinson."

Watching my father pacing about like a caged animal, I couldn't shake the feeling that this was some sort of test and one that I had to pass, though I wasn't exactly sure what he wanted from me.

"So what do you think, Nathan?"

"Sir, I think they are both capable of murder. We all are, for that matter, but as to whether James is telling the truth, I don't like him, or trust him. That doesn't necessarily mean he's lying." I spoke with care, wondering what my father wanted from me. Although I had said that, I knew he lied. My father was close to James' father and he wanted to trust him.

My father's expression was smooth, unyielding as I spoke and he looked at me speculatively, "Do you think that James had something to do with this?"

"Of that I can't be sure, Dad. I trust my instincts though and I think he did have something to do with it..." I stopped short of saying that I thought he was perhaps guiltier than Swinson, but I could see from my father's expression that this wasn't what he wanted to hear. His eyebrows pulled in together as I spoke and his mouth turned down as he surveyed me.

He leaned on his fingers, tapping them on his chin deep in thought as he watched me. The silence stretched on and on, neither of us speaking. I wasn't sure what to say and waited on my father to give me some queues as to where this conversation was leading. Eventually, after ten minutes of very uncomfortable silence my, father spoke, "Very well, Nathan. You are dismissed. Go back to your room and wait for me to get you..." Turning, I began walking away. My head swam with our conversation. As I reached the door handle, my father spoke again. "Do you not have something you would like to say to me?"

I swallowed hard, feeling as though I had a lump in my throat. I cleared my throat, "Sor..." I broke off, clearing my throat again and turned back towards him. He observed me without saying anything and I managed to speak clearly. "I am sorry about Saturday. I wish I could say something that would excuse my negligence, but I have nothing that will make it okay..."

"Thank you for your apology." Leaving the room, I felt like I could breathe again and I made my way back to my room. I caught sight of myself in the hallway mirror. I felt like I looked years older, as I worried about what would happen to Swinson, James, and me.

When I reached my bedroom door, I glanced across the landing and saw Nick sitting on the bed talking to Leanne. I smiled and went into my room, closing the door. I sat on my chair and smiled at how my brother and Leanne kept finding themselves back together.

CHAPTER 10
DREAMS AND DILEMMAS

While I sat on my bed, waiting to be summoned, I decided to get my iPod and listen to some Burnt Ashes as I tackled my math homework. I sat there on my bed with my books laid around me. I tried to work out a series of equations. I must have dozed off because I awoke in the woods. I lay on the ground with water dripping down on me. The woods were dark and the only light came from the moon overhead. I stared up and saw the branches swaying as a breeze flowed over me. I knew in some part of my mind I was dreaming, but I couldn't get myself to awaken. A part of me didn't want to face the world.

Directly ahead of me on the path was my dream girl. She looked at me as though she expected me. As I moved towards her, she turned and walked in the opposite direction. As the day slipped into night, I couldn't seem to catch up to her. I started to run, my heart pounding and my breath speeding as I chased after her. Every time I was almost level with her, something would stop me from reaching her. I groaned in frustration with myself for not being quick enough to catch her.

The first time I almost caught up with her a bolt of lightning crackled and a tree trunk fell into my path. Her laugh flowed around me like molten lava as I clambered over the tree towards her. I panted as I sped after her — I was so close! I reached out to touch her when suddenly my feet went under me and I landed hard on a patch of ice. I ignored the pain and forced myself to continue after her.

I kept going and was finally within touching distance. She stood right beside me. I could feel her heat, taste her breath on my tongue, and see her beautiful eyes as they lingered on mine. We stood near a cliff face, surrounded by trees with the sound of the sea rushing in the background. As she began speaking, the loudest crash sounded and I missed her words. I reached out to touch her, needing to feel her skin just once and my hand connected. I felt fireworks going off in my stomach and I moved closer to her, my hand leaving her face as I stood right in front of her. I wanted to touch her again, though she disappeared right before my eyes and I felt my world crumble. I felt my eyes tear up as I looked around for her, willing her to come back. Before I could properly look around, a hand touched my shoulder.

I awoke with a yelp, jumping a foot off the bed and felt my heart hammering in my chest. I had felt safe in the dream; here all I felt was uncertainty and fear.

I jumped up and saw my sister hovering over me. She looked startled by my reaction. "Sorry, I was having a bad dream. What's up, Jen?"

"You've been summoned to the barn." She spoke with an odd tone in her voice and I wondered what was wrong with her.

"What is it, Jen? What's wrong?"

"I'm not allowed to say yet. You'll see when we get... when we get to the barn." She turned away from me. Her hair was piled in a ponytail and she wore a black top with dark trousers.

She waited at the door for me as I gathered my things and placed them on the table. She leaned over me, seeming exasperated as she tugged the earpiece from my ear. I had forgotten I had it in and I put my music player on the desk and walked with her to the stairs in complete silence.

Before we reached the barn, Jenny turned and looked at me as though I had sprouted another head, but she didn't say a word. She just shook her head and led the way into the barn. She froze at the door and I stepped up beside her. I felt completely bewildered at what could have her behaving like a complete zombie.

The barn smelled normal, although some sort of oppressive force on the door caused me to stumble on my way inside. Once inside, I felt as though I was stripped back until the only emotion I could feel was vengeance. Walking further in, I stopped as I saw a bloody Swinson. He begged me for help with his streaming eyes; blood ran from his nose and lips and dripped onto his chest. He was tied up at the tree. The same tree they had whipped me against and I saw the whip on a table as my eyes darted about, trying to assimilate what was going on.

I froze upon seeing him and my father approached me. He stopped and said my name. I couldn't look at him. I watched my friend, transfixed as blood bubbled at the corner of his mouth and ran down his chin, to land on his chest.

"Nathan, speak to him; we have to find out why he killed the being before his sentence is carried out..."

The words *sentence* and *carried out* registered, and I turned to my father stunned, "Sentence?" I asked slowly. I was unable to comprehend what was happening. I had assumed he would be punished in much the same way as I was, but the way he was tied up and the way he looked at me suggested something much worse.

"Yes, Nathan. I had to sentence him to death. He will be beheaded at sundown so time is of the essence..."

"Why, why is he being killed?" I looked away from my father. My eyes darted back to Swinson as he spoke with anger colouring his tone at my questioning his orders.

"I had to agree to kill him, to stop the Beings from killing you. You see, they blame you for the murder of Allanus."

Finally, I understood why my father had been under so much pressure, though I couldn't understand why we hadn't fought them. We were stronger. We were more numerous and skilled than Black-Eyed Beings. Now wasn't the time to ask my father questions, although they burned my tongue like acid as I swallowed them back. I had little under two hours left to speak to my friend and we all needed answers.

I left my father's side and walked over to sit down beside Swinson.

"Hey, mate." He looked at me and shook.

"Nathan, I didn't kill that thing. I don't know what happened. You have to believe me." His voice broke as he stared at me with dread in his eyes.

"I do believe you, but I don't think my father has any choice though. Can you tell me what happened? In as much detail as you can remember. I need to know everything." I looked him in the eyes and choked as I realised that no matter what I did, he would still die and I was completely powerless to stop it. It was the first time in my whole life, I realised exactly how little power I had over my father and it sickened me.

"How far back should I go? Can you help me, Nathan?"

"I will try to help you. I promise, but I don't know what I can do." As I spoke, my gaze drifted over to my father. I saw him shake his head imperceptibly and my heart sank like a stone. I'd have to pretend that this might save him when, in fact, he was dead either way. He was being killed so I could live, which didn't seem reasonable to me at all. I had to move on; we had no time. I couldn't dwell on how unjust this was. I opened my mouth, swallowed the bile that threatened to rise, and asked him a question. "Start at the beginning; what happened at the ceremony?"

"James, Lucca, and I stood to the side, in the little room. It was stifling and James got us all a drink. Lucca didn't trust him and poured his on the plant in there when James wasn't looking. After a few minutes, we all came in and took our places. I don't remember much about the ceremony apart from the blood ritual."

"What about the knife?" I asked, watching as two of the council members walked into the barn towards my father. They whispered in his ear urgently. He shook his head once and turned back to me, urging me on with a wave of his hand.

"The knife... Oh yeah. Afterwards, we went back into the vestibule to wait until we were dismissed. Greg came in with the Ceremonial Blade and the Vessel to put them away. He started moaning about you. According to him, you had disgraced your father by leaving before your duties were all carried out." My cheeks burned as he spoke. I waved him on. "Lucca left first, going to meet up with Liam and Josh to plan something. I wasn't feeling very well and when I looked at the plant, I could see why. The plant was dead. I heard James speak to Greg, 'Only one of them took it.' And his father answered, 'Well, he'll take the blame, but if you can, teach Nathan a lesson. Our values should not be taken for granted, and he needs to learn these or step aside and allow you to become candidate.'"

I swung my head round and witnessed the half-shocked and half-enraged expression and I gulped. I would not like to be on the other side of that when he caught up with Greg.

"Okay, what happened next?"

His eyes darted about the barn as he answered me, "I don't remember much. I awoke in the woods, with the Ceremonial Blade at my side, covered in this sticky, purple goo. I wasn't sure where it came from. As I picked up the knife, some creatures stormed into the clearing and all eyes were on me." I nodded at him to continue as his eyes pleaded with me to help him. My body shook with nerves and I felt sick, but I needed to continue.

He swallowed and looked over at my dad before glancing back at me, whispering, "You can't do anything, can you? It looks like I'm guilty so I'll be punished?" His eyes filled with tears as I stared at my feet. "I'm gonna try, mate. I'll do all I can, but I can't promise anything." The tension in the room rose and my dad paced about, gesturing with his hands for me to get Swinson to continue. "Go on, Swin. What happened next?"

He took a deep breath and began speaking, his voice breaking on a few occasions as he recounted what had happened. "I noticed a pair of legs just outside the clearing, and I headed towards it. It was a body and as soon as they saw it, the creatures howled and screeched, so I turned and ran. I ran as far as I could, but I could hear them following me. My body shook and I slid under the fallen root of a tree, hiding there from those hunting me until our soldiers found me."

The soldiers. I kept repeating it in my head. *Demon foot soldiers.* Over and over again. We sat there side by side, as I tried to assimilate the fact that my father released those brutes to find him. I looked over towards him and he shook his head at me, motioning for me to move towards him. Our time was up. It made sense now, why Jenny was so upset. She had been seeing Swinson on and off for years and they cared about each other.

I turned back to him and gave him a swift pat on the shoulder, my shoulders shaking as I tried to suppress how hard it was to leave my friend there with a death sentence hanging over him. I re-joined my father, but stumbled as he called out, "Nathan, please. Please help me." My head thudded painfully and I had to swallow a few times as I walked. I turned and gave him a stiff nod, to let him know I had heard him, but I knew with certainty that there was nothing I could do. My father's word was law and if I didn't want the same fate, there was nothing I could do.

I reached my father and he nodded at two soldiers I hadn't noticed standing beside the tree. They untied Swinson and dragged him out of the barn. I stood there feeling nothing but shame. If I had put the knife away, all of this could have been avoided.

This was all my fault and now one of my best friends was going to be killed because of my carelessness.

"Come with me." My father commanded, breaking through my thoughts, and I followed, unable to feel anything as we walked towards the clearing in a detached numbness, just putting one foot in front of the other. I knew that the only reason Swinson was to die was so I could live and I didn't know how to live with that. I didn't know if I could live with it. How do I live with the fact that someone had been murdered so I could live? He was being sacrificed for me. We reached the entrance to the woods and followed a path I knew well, one I had been dreaming about that afternoon. We headed towards the stone clearing in the centre of the woods.

As we reached the clearing, I saw Nick and Leanne holding hands. Jenny was also there, standing stiff as a board next to my mother, who looked at me through pursed lips. I also spotted more faces dotted throughout the gathering. Swinson's parents, his older sister, and younger brother all gathered, although his other little sister was absent. Joe's face stood out, his bruises healing, now purple in places, but tinged with black. Lucca stood straight-backed and proud, next to his father and older brothers.

Then I saw James and my insides boiled, with lava flowing through my veins. Both he and his father stood there with the most insincere expressions on their faces, but I knew now was not the time for vengeance. I would get him. I would make him pay for the murder of my friend. He would not get away with it. As I glared at him, his eyes flickered over to mine for a brief moment and he smirked at me. I began moving until Nick put his hand on my arm, holding me in place.

Swinson was led forward and pushed down over a stone. My father walked over and glanced around the clearing before he nodded to the trees. I followed his gaze and could see the Beings standing there, watching the proceedings with interest. My father spoke and although his words rang clear, disgust coloured his tone, which made me think he was less than happy with this sentence.

"Swinson Daniels, you have been found guilty of murdering a Being and have been sentenced to death. May your blood salt the earth and may your death remind us that loyalty is our most important virtue. It is in fact more important than life or truth." With that, his hands transformed into claws and he swiped his hands down and severed Swinson's head until it came off clean. The snapping of bone sounded like the grating of a saw shattering the silence, going right through me. I shook with every cut and the pouring of blood as the head came loose, making me nauseous. I could feel the bile rising from my stomach. I watched his body writhe and shake for a few seconds. I wanted to look away so badly. I knew if I looked away, I would show weakness and I would probably be forced to face a similar fate. I stood and watched with my face a mask of disinterest until it was finally over.

He wiped his claws on a handkerchief handed to him by Greg and everyone departed. I observed my father walk over to the Daniels family. He spoke to them, his hand placed on Liam's shoulder in a show of support. I watched for a few seconds as Liam and my father conversed in low whispers. Linda left with the younger two children and I glanced down again at the body of my friend, tears clouding my vision as I turned my back on him. I headed back to the house, desperate to get back to normality and forget about all of this.

I turned around and headed over to the clearing by the cliffs. I needed some time alone to process everything that had happened. I walked along, not feeling the biting wind or the raindrops that had started and soon I was drenched. My body shivered, but I ignored the feeling. I kept walking, faster and faster as footsteps crunched behind me. I spun around ready to take out the person who had come up behind me, when I saw it was just Lisa.

"Hey baby, are you ok?" she crooned at me and I wanted to shoot myself for responding, but I needed her in that moment. I said nothing and grabbed her hand, pulling her roughly along with me. She shivered and I wasn't sure if it was the cold or pleasure that I was holding her hand. I actually didn't care. "Nathan," her voice came out in a shout, over the roaring wind, which was getting louder and louder as we neared the cliff face. "Where are you taking me?"

I shrugged at her, but I knew where we were headed and I smiled tightly as I thought about her distracting me. She stopped and pulled on my arm to stop me. I wanted to keep walking, "Nathan, stop!" Her voice commanded me to stop and I spun around and looked at her with venom. "I need you, Lisa, right now, but if you don't wanna be here then please feel free to FUCK OFF!"

Her eyes went as wide as saucers and she licked her lips, smiling at me. "Fine, don't bite my fucking head off." She pulled me along and we finally reached the cliff face. I shimmied us along the edge to the overlapping trees. We ducked under the branches and she turned towards me, like a cat stalking prey. Her eyes were hungry and as she stalked towards me, I winced as a memory of earlier hit me.

Lisa came closer and stood beside me, running her fingers through my hair. I smiled and spoke through my teeth, "Make me forget, Lisa." Her lips found mine and her hungry kisses drove me wild as she backed me up against a tree. My back burned and my chest hurt, but her kissing me helped keep everything I felt under wraps. My body responded to her and as her cold hands snaked under my t-shirt, I shivered. She smiled at me and stuck her tongue into my mouth. I pulled her tighter against me and slipped my fingers inside her top. Her groan made me want more. I turned so she faced the tree. As we turned, she looked up at me, licked her lips, and kissed my neck. I was burning and then as I was getting into it, the girl's face popped into my head and my desire snuffed out like a light.

77

I rested my head on Lisa's and kissed the top of her head. "Can we just sit, and watch the water?"

She groaned and nodded her head, but not before muttering, "Sometimes I really hate you, Nathan." I laughed at her and we sat at the edge of the cliff, sheltered a little from the howling wind and driving rain.

"Lisa, why did you come after me?" I asked, hoping she hadn't seen how weak I was being. Her questioning look caused the hairs on my arm to prickle up and I looked out at the water.

"Nathan, he was one of your best friends. I had to see if you were okay. Swinson was a great guy and..."

I spun towards her and all but screamed at her to leave, "GET AWAY FROM ME, RIGHT NOW, LISA!" She scuttled backwards in fright and I shook my head, "DEMONS DO NOT FEEL, YOU FUCKING KNOW THAT. IF YOU CAME HERE EXPECTING TO GRIEVE OR WHATEVER THE FUCK MORTALS DO, THEN YOU CAME TO THE WRONG PLACE."

My chest was rising and falling rapidly and she turned and walked out of the clearing, "Nathan, you are a complete arse, you know that, right?"

As she walked away, my walls came down and I felt as though my chest hurt, but I shook it off and walked home ten minutes after her, needing to get into my bed and sleep off whatever these stupid feelings were. I had never felt like that before and I didn't know if I was broken or just weak; I wasn't behaving like a normal Demon.

That night as I drifted off, I thought of the girl and fell into a deep sleep for a few hours, until I dreamed of her. Her long black hair swished behind her and she turned and smiled at me, before walking into my arms. "Welcome home, baby," she whispered in my ear and her arms closed around me, warming me at first, then burning. I awoke in a cold sweat, alone in my room in the middle of the night.

CHAPTER 11
SHOCK & AWE

The rest of the night passed as slept in a fitful doze. I woke several times due to nightmares about writhing bodies covered in blood. The blood would turn into lava and burn through my skin. I must have awakened more than a dozen times before I finally dropped off into a deep sleep. The last time I checked my clock it was four a.m. As I drifted into a deep sleep, I saw her face and it offered me some comfort. In my dream, she moved closer to me and sat beside me, whispering in my ear.

"Sleep now, Nathan. It's okay, baby. I'm here; now you can sleep." I felt the tension leave me as I drifted deeper, where there were no bodies on the ground and no girls comforting me.

Later that morning, Nick came in and shook me awake, looking as tired as I felt. "Nate, it's time to get up for school."

My eyes rolled. The events of the last few days weighed me, pressing me into the mattress. At least, I now had a better understanding of the phrase, 'Burning the candle at both ends.' I felt completely burnt out. Nick left and stopped at the door, "Dad's waiting on us all, so you better hurry."

I forced myself to sit up. I rubbed my hands over my face to rub the memory of Swinson's execution away, but I couldn't. I went into the shower and turned the water temperature up until it was scalding hot. The shower was so hot that little red welts appeared on my skin as I stood under the water. The burning sensation of the water on my skin distracted me from all the noise inside my head.

Finally, I got out of the shower and looked in the mirror. My dark hair curling and messy. As I studied my reflection in the mirror, one of the Beings appeared, glaring at me. After a split second, it was gone and I hoped it was my imagination; the alternative was too scary to contemplate. I double-checked the mirror as I left the bathroom, but the Being had definitely vanished.

As I pulled my jeans on and stifled a yawn, Jenny burst into the room. She looked disappointed to see me up and the upset girl from the previous day was replaced with what looked like a more vicious version of my sister.

"Aww, you're up. Dad says you have to hurry up. He wants to speak to you before he leaves for work."

She bounced out of my room as I pulled my top over my head. I noticed that I had picked clothes that were completely different colours. My casual was blue and my jumper jade green. I realised I had to change one of them so I walked over to my drawers and pulled out a dark blue jumper. I focused on the smallest details because I was so tired and completely overwhelmed with the events of the past week. My mind was in freefall and this was my way of trying to control a situation beyond my control.

After a few minutes, I was ready. I grabbed my school stuff and stuffed them into my backpack. I grabbed my mobile, which I hadn't seen since Friday and my water bottle, and threw both of them into my bag as I ran towards the stairs.

I skidded into the dining room and paused in the doorway as most of my family gathered there, waiting for me.

"Finally," Nick muttered almost under his breath. My father stood as I made my way into the room, choosing to sit beside Nick and Jenny.

"Swinson was executed yesterday and today, you both return to school. I want you to stop anyone from speaking about the events of the weekend. The mortals must not find out, so there will be no speaking about it at all in public. Is that understood?"

"Yes, sir."

"Okay. On another note, our sacrifice will arrive in a few days. Nick, she'll be in your old room for the time being and Nathan," he looked directly at me, as though seeing through me. "You will protect her at all costs. She is not to be harmed. As candidate, this is your most important responsibility." I nodded at him, not trusting myself to speak. My thoughts raced a mile a second. So *I was to be this thing's babysitter. Oh that sounds just fanfuckingtastic.*

"You are dismissed. Nathan, wait a moment." We stood side by side, watching as everyone else filed out the room and headed into the kitchen. My father eventually looked at me, "This weekend has been tough on you. You must remember you are Demon and our heritage will help you through it. Trust in our blood and know the strength inside you is stronger than any of the prospective candidates. I know Swinson was your friend, but I couldn't let the murder of a Being go unpunished. If I did, there would be open war on all Demons and you, my son, would be the first target." Nodding again and feeling like a little dog in a car, my father spoke again, his voice sounding vicious, "I know that Swinson wasn't responsible. Jack checked out the plant in the vestibule and Swinson told the truth. I will catch Greg and James, and they will be punished." His face as he spoke was murderously angry and as he continued, a dark light ruminated from behind him. "They will not get away with this and your friend's death will not be in vain. His father knows that I will be working to exonerate him." I saw something in the window from the corner of my eye. When I looked, I could see her face gazing in impassively. She vanished after a moment, although my heart raced at the glimpse of her. From the corner of my eye, I saw my father check his watch as I gazed transfixed at the window. My father clapped me on the shoulder and when I looked over at him, he smiled at me. "I'm off. Get Jenny and head to school. No more skiving, Nathan. I mean it."

As he left, I realised that this was the first time in what felt like years that he had put his hand on me in an affectionate way. He usually punished me or didn't show any interest at all. Nick and Jenny, he was openly affectionate. With me, though, he always seemed closed off.

We walked to school in silence. After a while, Joe joined us, but didn't speak and eventually we made our way into school. Seeing James ahead joking and laughing with Matty, Joshua, and Aiden had my blood boiling. Joe looked at me and I turned away, although fury raced through me painfully.

Ignoring the rage inside me, I walked through the school doors, but not before a throw away comment reached me, "...beat up and whipped, his father has de-Demoned him cause he's a little bitch..." I turned towards him, my eyes turning black as Joe stepped in front of me.

"Don't do that dick any favours; he'll get his. Nate, don't let him get to you. He wants you exposed and as soon as he gets what he wants, he wins."

I calmed myself by first focusing on my shaking hands and then forcing calmness I didn't really feel through my body as I walked. I wanted to rip his head off, but I knew what he was trying to do. I wanted to get him and tell him to be afraid. I didn't know how I would do it, but I would figure it out somehow.

School passed in a blur and that night, I spent my time catching up on all the work I had missed. The following day, an opportunity presented itself to me and I couldn't resist getting my message across to that fucker.

James walked a little ahead of me during class time. It looked as if he headed to the library. He didn't notice me as I looped around the corridor and caught him before he entered, pushing him into a disused office. I slammed him full force up against the wall and put my arm over his throat. I allowed my hands to morph into claws, holding them at a vein in his throat as fury pulsed through me.

I froze him with my powers. I could feel his powers trying to find a way around mine. I brushed them aside, as though they were no more than a fly in my face. Demon power raced through me and I stood tall before spitting out, "I know what you did and I know what you are trying to do. You won't succeed. For every single time you try, I will ruin something you care about. You are not getting away with this; I will make sure of it..." I broke off and turned my hand back to normal before I punched him full force in the nose. I relished the sound of the bone breaking. He would heal it in seconds, though he wouldn't be able to get rid of the blood from Demon sight. Strolling towards the door, I called over my shoulder, "Mop yourself up, you disgusting piece of filth."

The rest of the day sped by and the next few days at school followed without incident, although I spotted James watching me occasionally. His eyes burned through me, as I smiled and ignored him. I knew I couldn't react. Although I wasn't afraid of him, I was wary of him. He would keep trying to come after me and I would need to be on guard to make sure he didn't succeed.

***

That evening, my father called a meeting. Since it was Thursday, the sacrifice was due to arrive the following day. I walked into the meeting my thoughts circling around to James and I was distracted as I took my seat at the dining table. My eyes on the water jug in front of me, as I wondered how to stop James and get rid of him, once and for all. He was like an itch that I wanted to scratch badly.

A hand touched my shoulder and I looked round in surprise to see Jack standing there. He was frowning at me as he took a seat to my left. My father walked in followed by the rest of my family and I took a deep breath in, making an effort to concentrate on the meeting and not drift into my head.

My father cleared his voice and everyone sat down. He began speaking, but looked only at me and it unnerved me. I felt as though my teeth were on edge as he went through a few demon housekeeping rules. No mortals in school and to be careful because there was a new police officer poking around. My head drifted and I thought of the girl I was dreaming about as I turned and looked out the window.

"Nathan, are you listening to me?" My fathers' stern voicebroke into my head and I shook my head wanting to clear it of her.

"Sorry," my voice came out small and my hands started to shake under the table. I was worried about what they were going to do. "Pay attention, Nathan. This is important."

I nodded and refocused on my dad as he started speaking,

"The sacrifice arrives tomorrow and Nathan, you will have to look out for her. Keep an eye on her at school and watch your friends around her."

I nodded at him, but my look must have been confused because he continued,

"She will envoke their primal instincts and they will want to hurt her.

You are too young to remember Martha, but when she was Nick's candidate, he had to save her life at least seven times and it looks like this girl is much more powerful so you will have your hands full."

I looked at him in horror, wondering what would happen if I failed to keep an eye on this stupid fucking mortal and my dad answered my unspoken question.

"You won't fail. A Stevenson has never, ever failed in protecting a sacrifice. The most dangerous times are full moons and the Halloween period, but as long as you are around her, she should be safe."

With that he stood and walked out, my family following behind. I sat there stunned, staring after them and not realising that Jack was still sitting beside me.

"Relax, kiddo. You'll be fine." I turned and looked at him and he smiled over at me, clapping his hand on my shoulder, "you ready to get your ass whipped at GTA?"

I pushed my chair back and laughed, "bring it old man. You haven't won a single game yet." As we left the room, my body began to relax and I realised I would just need to be prepared for whatever the next day brought. I would need to stay vigilant and make sure that the sacrifice was safe, but I could still enjoy my life.

Friday evening dawned and I sat in the rarely used lounge playing gin rummy with my brother and sister while we waited on the sacrifice to arrive. My father was home from work in his office and my mother pottered about in the kitchen.

After half an hour as we heard a car on the driveway, Nick got up to check it out and beckoned Jenny over. I busied myself by tidying up the cards as Nick said, "It's Julie and the sacrifice. Oh my God, the sacrifice looks like a deer caught in headlights, all doe eyed and innocent."

Julie was our family's social worker. It had been decided years ago that it would look very suspicious if we had too many Demons in social work, so each one of ours had four or five Demon families to serve. I had met her a few times over the years; she always looked the same and I wasn't a big fan of her. I stood and walked to the front door with my family. I wasn't really looking at the car, not bothered at all about who the sacrifice was. I felt bored already of the stupid ceremony that happened every time we got a new sacrifice. The only part I looked forward to was the celebration of the sacrifice's arrival later on tonight. It was always a party and usually good fun.

I heard the car door open, looked over automatically as she stepped out of the car. The girl I had been dreaming about for weeks, she was our sacrifice.

My thoughts all scattered and I felt like I had been punched in the stomach, all my breath left me. I understood just from a cursory glance at her Nick's deer comment, and the thought almost made me laugh aloud.

I felt like we had already met. I knew her face from every angle and knew what her voice would sound like before she even spoke. Her face was perfect, even though she looked terrified and I was completely consumed by her eyes. I felt a surge of fire shoot through me as she looked into mine. In a single glance, she had wiped out my history, my heritage and she burned through me, igniting my heart and soul in an inferno of emotion.

The moment I looked at her, I felt like my world had stopped, as if it tilted beneath my feet, as though her small glance at me had torn apart everything I was. Her eyes consumed me and my head swam with confusion. As I turned with my family, I stumbled on the step. I barely noticed because all I wanted to do was turn and look at her again, to see if she was actually real.

The End

DEMONS THROUGH TIME

In the beginning, before there were Demons, Lucifer was expelled from Heaven. While on Earth, he met and fell in love with Gweneviere and they had three children. He gave her an unnaturally long life and their children lived until they were three hundred and fifty years old. Just before the children passed, Lucifer and Gweneviere decided to go to the underworld and take the souls off all mortals who had committed sins and did not repent with them. They became the King and Queen of Hell.

The King and Queen of Hell returned to Earth when their children died as they could not reproduce in Hell and their three children were reborn. When the children were reborn, Lucifer decided to find the descendants of the Children of Angels. When one of these children was found, the Demons would have a feast on a specific date, October thirty-first, as this was the date that their souls shone brightest. Consuming their souls on this day would sustain them for a full year.

Some of the souls of the Descendants shone brighter than others, and it was prophesied in the seventh century that these Descendants would, if they lived past eighteen years old, have powers, which could destroy Demons and their families. It became even more imperative that the Descendants were found and Demon colonies appeared as the children of the three Demons procreated with desirable humans and produced more Demon offspring, though none as powerful as the three Demon children born of Lucifer and Gweneviere.

Not all Descendants were found and the Demon Elders would die every six hundred years, although they didn't age at all. The essences of the Descendants made sure that the elders stayed young and healthy until one day they would just not wake up.

For nineteen hundred years, this cycle repeated and the Demons grew stronger with each reproduction. In the 1900s, when the Demons were reborn, a prophecy was made that this would be the last cycle of their rebirth. As the Demon children got older, Lewis was the oldest and made the Chief of all Demons on Earth. Lilith, angry at the fact that her older brother had been made Chief by their father, she disregarded the rules about not having more than one mortal per family per year. She rebelled after fifty years in this cycle on Earth. Jack, the youngest was the most humane of the three Elder Demons and although he enjoyed the feasts at Halloween, he did not take pleasure in torturing mortals the way his brother and sister did. He was quite happy to follow the directives from his father. In 1984, Lucifer and Gwen made their journey back to Hell, having been on Earth since 1950.

It had been decided that Lewis, Lilith, and Jack would all take on public service jobs when they arrived, as this would help them meet more Descendents and find the ones with the most luminous souls to be devoured.

Lewis met Emma in 1975 and married her in 1979. In 1980, Nickolas was born followed by Nathan in 1984 and Jennifer in 1985. While Emma was pregnant with Nathan, a great friend of Lewis' came back to visit and prophesied that one of their children would betray them. Since Emma was pregnant with Nathan, they decided that it was Nathan, and decided to be harder on him to make sure his humanity was quashed from him.

Humanity would break them and would cause betrayal. Little did they know that their treatment of Nathan would lead to his betraying them by falling in love with their sacrifice. To find out more about Nathan and the sacrifice, read *Escaping Demons Saga, Luminosity* and *Candlelight*.

Coming soon find out more about Nathan and Jasmine in:

Escaping Demons Saga: Luminosity
Here is a sneak peek into their world.

PROLOGUE

Have you ever been so scared that you wish you had never been born? That all your life's experiences are just your imagination? That we really were just puppets on a string being made to do things by stronger forces than our own initiative or imagination? Have you ever felt that you won't survive the next day, hour, or even minute?

Or had all your life force draining from you as you give up the fight for life because life doesn't feel worth living? Trusting someone only for him to betray you at a time when you need him the most?

I have, and it was the most terrifying experience of my life.

My name is Jasmine Johnstone and I was seventeen years old when this happened. I've been an orphan since the age of five, when my parents died in a car accident that I mysteriously survived. I've always been a little bit odd because I have a sort of sixth sense and can read people pretty well. My mum called me her "little oracle." She told me I was special and so sensitive that I picked up on imprints of souls of the dearly departed.

My mum had been a nurse and my dad a surgeon at the same hospital as each other. I remember her telling me that my dad had swept her off her feet and would send her a rose after every time he worked with her, or saw her at work. Then the accident happened and my happy little family was torn apart. I've always remembered the exact day they died, as it happened the day before my fifth birthday. The day of my birthday dawned and there was no cake, balloons, or celebration, just a lonely hospital room with no visitors. I cried myself to sleep remembering how sweet my parents had been and awoke to the familiar smell of roses surrounding me, but when I looked around the room, there were none.

All I've ever remembered about the accident was the feeling of flying through the air. I remembered crying for my mum and dad to help me. I was stuck and couldn't see anything. The sound of my crying alerted those on the scene that there was life in the car. We never made it to my grandparents — they didn't want me when the courts offered, neither did any of my extended family. I had no idea why nobody wanted me. I couldn't have known that there were sinister forces at work, turning the intentions of family members against me and leaving me an unwanted outcast shunted into foster care.

When I first went into care, I was labelled a "special case." Although I was placed near the area I had begun my childhood in, I had none of my own belongings, as my new foster family didn't want me to have anything that would remind me of my parents. They were worried it would upset me and thought it was best for me, but it still hurt.

In the end, I felt like I was being passed about from house to house, from family to family. I never stayed with one for more than a few years. The experience was confusing and lonely, and eventually resulted in my refusing to speak to anyone for a long time. I found I was able to communicate my needs perfectly well with crude gestures and facial expressions. Even then, the interest in me was so minimal that this self-imposed silence was only deemed as an attempt at drawing attention to myself. Didn't they see I didn't want attention? I just wanted to belong. Eventually my mutism passed and I finally made my first friend, Gwen, who became my lifeline at the home I had eventually been placed in. Although she was only ten years old, she was so much more mature than I was.

We were always in trouble with, not only the people who ran the home, but also with the other children who were in the home. They always got away with whatever they did to us; being very pretty with fair hair and innocent faces made them, in the eyes of the wardens, unaccountable. So even though we were picked on, had food thrown at us, were beaten and called names, we were happy because we had each other. We would play in the gardens until sundown, and then go in for dinner. We would sneak our food from the main cafeteria into the cupboard beside the drawing room at every meal.

We generally managed to avoid the bullies most of the time, but there was one time when they attacked Gwen and I snapped. I went for the main bully and flew at her, knocking her down onto the grass. My fists flew as I punched her hard on the mouth, in the stomach, and scratched at her arms as she had clawed at my hair. When she cried on the ground, I got up and attacked another girl who had made my life hell. She ended up with a broken arm. I didn't mean to be so vicious to those girls, but I just couldn't take it anymore. They left us alone after that.

A few weeks after that incident, we were both moved on. I went to stay with the Greene family while Gwen went to stay with her aunt. I was twelve at the time and completely devastated at the loss of my first friend. I was a "monster child" to the Greenes at first, but the love and kindness they showed me broke down my mistrust, and I grew to love living with them. Then, after almost five years of living with them, my world was shattered.

I had just come home with a friend from school to find a familiar face standing at the living room window. My heart dropped to my shoes, and I knew without a shadow of a doubt I would be moving on soon. The Greenes sat in tears as I walked into the room. They looked directly at me, misery etched into their lined faces. Julie, my social worker, stood there at the window and watched our silent exchange. When she spoke, she couldn't look me in the eye. She seemed frustrated, which came across in her tone and in the clipped words she spoke to me.

"You're moving again."

I nodded at her, and asked the obvious question. "Why?"

"I don't know. Don't ask stupid questions. Say your goodbyes and get ready."

"When am I moving?" Tears stung my eyes, but I had it ingrained in me that I wouldn't cry. In care homes, the first to cry was labelled the weakest and was always picked on, so I rarely cried in front of people. No matter how much they hurt me, I very rarely cried. Dawn's eyes watered and Martin looked at me in dismay while we all watched the social worker.

"Next week," she snapped. "I'll be off now." With that, she picked up her bag and stormed from the room, slamming the door on her way out.

As soon as the door closed, Mrs Greene walked over to me and pulled me into a hug. I reciprocated gratefully, but nothing could quieten the questions that rolled around inside my head.

I thought they wanted me. I was finally safe here. Oh my God, I'm gonna miss everyone so much...

"We did want you, Jasmine," Mrs Greene sobbed into my shoulder, "but they wouldn't let us keep you. We fought so hard but the judge overruled us. We'll keep fighting though, I promise."

I stood there feeling more than numb. Anger licked at me as I realised that they had known I was being moved on for a while, but hadn't said anything to me. I was gutted but I knew they meant well. As I disentangled myself from Dawn, Martin caught my eye and whispered, "We didn't want to tell you until we had a definitive answer. We have one more chance but if it falls through, there will be nothing we can do. I'm so sorry, honey."

I nodded at him and walked up to my room. As soon as the door closed, I broke down. I would miss this house and their family who had adopted me as one of their own since I had arrived.

The Greenes tried to appeal for the right for me to stay, but they were refused. For the most part, I was numb, destroyed to be leaving a family that loved me, and my friends behind. There was no explanation given, just that it wasn't possible for me to remain living there.

CHAPTER 1
MOVING ON

The following weekend I sat in a car, driving away from the only real home I'd ever known to God only knew where. I never thought for a moment that this drive would see my life put in danger, or see some of my worst nightmares come to life.

As we arrived at my new home, my jaw dropped in surprise — the place was amazing! We drove down a long driveway towards an old-fashioned farmhouse with trees lining an expansive garden. The barn was the most unusual part of the grounds, as there was a massive tree growing through the middle of the structure, which towered out of the roof. A family, my new family, stood at the bottom of the steps of the house, ready to greet us.

"The Stevensons," imparted my social worker.

A man and a woman, who were obviously the mother and father, stood at the front of the welcoming group. He was gorgeous, with light brown hair and a chiselled jaw line. The mother was beautiful, with long coal-black hair and a stern mouth. Behind them were three teenagers close to my age group. The oldest, close to twenty, looked just like his mother, with dark hair. He was very handsome, but his face was distorted with an ugly glaring frown. The girl standing next to him looked around my age or slightly older, with curly brown hair and a blank, bored expression on her face. The last boy turned away from the car, looking across the lawn. He was no older than seventeen. He had twinkling green eyes set in a gentle face. Something about him drew me in, like electricity or magnetism. I tingled when I looked at him, surprising me. I wasn't interested in boys — I just wanted a home of my own, somewhere I belonged.

As we stepped out of the car, the family stared at us and Mr Stevenson spoke, "Julie, how nice to see you. Please follow us!" The whole family turned as one, which was slightly creepy, and beckoned us into their home. As we walked up the steps, Mr Stevenson indicated we should go into the large lounge area just inside the front door.

As I walked, I wondered what was going to happen to me and how I would survive another new family, new rules, and another new life. Moving to a new home should have been normal for me by now, but each time a family rejected me still felt like a punch in the stomach. Each time I thought, this family will want me, they will want to keep me, but they never did. Only the Greenes wanted me, and for some reason, I was taken from them. Sometimes, most of the time, I felt unwanted and lonely.

Instead of moping, I looked around the room and took in my surroundings — the place seemed nice enough, the living room was cream with wooden flooring, and through the patio doors was a large garden. I noticed just how extensive the grounds were as I stared out of the window morosely. *At least I will have space while I was here.*

As I glanced around the living room, the boy caught my eye again. I wasn't sure what it was, instinct, intuition, or whatever, but something made me want to trust him. As I sat trying to figure that out, I realised he looked at me as though he had seen me before or something, and was trying to place where. I quickly looked away as a jolt of that same electricity zapped through me. I felt slightly overwhelmed and intimidated by his stare. I continued looking around the room, my eyes landing on a luminous, red, urn-shaped vase and I stared at that for a few moments before abruptly swiping my head round to the middle of the room, suddenly aware that everyone in the room looked at me, waiting on an answer to something someone had just said. There was a short, awkward pause, after which Mr Stevenson continued.

"When you're living in this house, I expect you to uphold our standards. You will strive to succeed in school and achieve the grades we have come to expect from our children. Lateness will not be accepted, nor will untidiness."

I gazed impassively at him as my brain tried to digest what he said. He hadn't said anything kind or welcoming, just barked out orders. When it was clear I had no response, he merely continued with his orders.

"You will walk to school every day with Nathan," and as he said this, he nodded to the boy directly next to me, who watched me with an unwavering stare and half-smiled at me, "and Jenny," he concluded, nodding this time to the girl on my left. As I looked at her with a smile, I was shocked by the venomous glare that consumed her face. Suddenly I felt quite upset, and realised that I was hoping my last foster home would be a nice one, but if the look on Jenny's face was anything to go by, I had a suspicion that kind and loving wouldn't be an option.

The atmosphere in the room changed slightly as Mr Stevenson and his wife talked to the social worker responsible for dropping me off, Julie. She was small, with auburn hair and pretty brown eyes, the colour of tree bark. She was very cold at times, aloof almost, and when she suddenly stood to leave, I felt a pang of fear. I couldn't quite shake off the feeling of foreboding her leaving left me with. As she walked to the door, terror raced through me; I didn't really want her to go. In fact, from the looks I had just received, I wanted to go with her.

She smiled softly at me from the door and I felt a sad sense of farewell. I turned my head around and gazed back around the sitting room, where the new... my new family gathered.

As my gaze touched Mr Stevenson, he stated, "Well, Jasmine, welcome to our home. I am Mr Lewis Stevenson; you may call me Sir or Mr Stevenson. My wife is Emma, but you may call her Ma'am or Mrs Stevenson. Our children you can call by name, Nicholas who is twenty-one, Nathan who is seventeen next week and Jennifer who is sixteen." He looked around at his children and pointed out each one, but they seemed completely uninterested in me, although Nathan kept glancing at me and away again. It was as though he was trying to figure something out, but I had no idea what it was. Mr Stevenson continued speaking, "I expect you'd like to see your room? Nathan will show you where to go. You can unpack and settle in, and then come down for dinner at six."

He turned away from me in dismissal, so I took note of the looks on each person's face at this point. The older boy, Nicholas, looked annoyed; Jenny had a look of disgust on her face. And the mother exuded unhappiness. I was so confused. What had I missed? It was almost as if someone had died and I was intruding or something. Before I had a chance to figure it out, Nathan rose to his feet and, with a look of pure confusion on his face, picked up my bags and walked towards the stairs at the back of the entranceway. Rather than continuing to deal with the hostility in the room, I quickly got to my feet and followed him up the stairs and into a cold dark-panelled room.

The room had two large windows, one smallish wardrobe, a chest of drawers, and a double bed. He dropped my bag on the floor, turned around, and walked out of the room without saying anything at all. I wondered if the family had some kind of custom I didn't know about and I had offended them. Or if they just didn't like strangers in their house. I hadn't missed when Mr Stevenson said, "Welcome to our home..." Although his tone suggested anything but welcome — perhaps I wasn't wanted here and had been foisted on this family. The thought depressed me and made me miss my home with the Greenes. I made a mental note to try to question them later on, but decided to focus on unpacking since that was what I was up here to do. I couldn't get the boy out of my head. What had that been when I first set eyes on him? I never did that. Why now? Why him? As these thoughts circled around in my head, I pulled out my iPod and turned Bon Jovi on full volume to drown out my thoughts while I took in my new surroundings.

The room had a bit of a creepy vibe, with no pictures or mirrors, or any personal touches at all. I opened the wardrobe and emptied my clothes bag on the bed, but before I unpacked it, I really needed to find a bathroom. I left the room and immediately spotted Nathan standing at the doorway of another room. I was about to go over to ask him where the nearest bathroom was when I heard a voice telling him that something was "evil" and "only a sacrifice."

"...Jasmine's trying to drag you in, make you feel. You have to fight it,

Nathan. Do not let her destroy you and everything you stand for. Conniving little cow." I felt stunned by the malice in the voice, which was intense enough that I decided to forgo asking where the bathroom was and instead find it myself. I searched along the hallway, randomly opening doors. Eventually, after two open doors, three bedrooms, and two closed doors, I found a smallish bathroom. I had just walked in when Jenny stormed out of her own room, yelling at me, "What are you doing in my bathroom? Get out NOW!"

I looked at her for a few stunned seconds before I finally managed to stammer, "W-where is the nearest bathroom for me to use?"

She merely growled at me, muttered something incoherent, and walked away, leaving me and Nathan, who had been following her, standing in the hall. As he watched me, a strange sort of electricity flowed through me again and my heart thrummed at the sight of him in front of me. He nodded his head towards my room and led the way into the room and over to a door I hadn't seen since the open door from the wardrobe had been blocking it. He turned on the light to reveal a small bathroom complete with lavatory, sink, and shower. I started to thank him, but he had already left the room, making sure to slam the door on his way out. What was with these people, screaming at me for going into a bathroom, slamming doors, not speaking? It gave me a headache, and as I walked further into the bathroom, I admitted to myself that it also unnerved me slightly.

I put my toiletry bag onto the sink shelf and noticed that there was no soap or towels in the room, which could prove to be a problem considering I may want to use the shower at some point. They had clearly known I was coming to stay with them, so why hadn't they put anything in here for me to use? I wasn't sure if I should go and ask about it; I had clearly been told to come down only for dinner at six. I couldn't help thinking this was some kind of strange test. I looked in the mirror above the sink, shocked to see a pale face staring back at me. She had dark circles under her eyes that made her seem tired, but her eyes were alert and wary. She looked scared. I watched as her upper teeth snuck out and grazed her lower lip. She looked like she was cracking up. For all I knew, maybe I was. I slumped down onto the toilet lid with my head in my hands. I couldn't shake the feeling that something was wrong. Every instinct in my body screamed at me to run through the trees at the edge of the garden and never look back. It was crazy! What possible reason could I have had to be scared of this family? They seemed normal enough, if a bit stingy with household provisions.

I had two bags with me, one filled with clothes that were now all over the bed and another with shoes and odds and ends. I only owned four pairs of shoes, so it didn't take me long to unpack them. It took about five minutes to put all of my clothes away, and as I turned to sort through my other items, I noticed the window had been left open. I looked out and saw I was in the room overlooking the left-hand side of the house, facing the garden, trees, and a path. I itched to investigate that path, but that would be something I'd need to do in the daytime since it looked quite old and it was going to be dark soon. The last thing I needed was to break my ankle, or my neck, on my first night here. I turned around and finished getting myself sorted. The room looked much better with my little bits and pieces scattered around. I placed my three picture frames on the drawers, the one of the Greenes and myself, the one of myself and Gwen, and one of myself and my parents, taken when I was four years old. I was completely drained and when I looked at my watch, it was twenty to five. I had plenty of time before dinner, so I decided to lie down for a while and get myself together. I fell asleep looking at the faces of the people who had loved me, and dreamed of being wrapped in their arms. My mother gave me a knowing look as she handed me a rose, the thorns pricking my fingers and causing me to wince in my sleep. The smell of roses filled the room, and for the first time since I had turned five, I could smell the pungent aroma. The smell was a comfort to me as I began to stir, but was so comforting that I felt myself relax back into my dream and nod back off to sleep.

An hour later the sound of my bedroom door banging off the wall frightened me and I awoke with a jolt. It felt like the whole room shuddered with the force of the bang.

"Oi! It's dinnertime. Get up," a voice from the doorway shouted.

I jumped about a mile off the bedspread and scrambled to get up. I wondered whether this family was always this short with people they had just met, or if it was just me. Nathan and Nicholas watched me, so I got up much faster than I normally would, slipped my shoes on, and stumbled my way out of the door.

I glanced at my watch and saw it was twenty to six. They had told me dinner would be at six. Why would they wake me up like that if it weren't time yet? Confusion engulfed me and my relaxed feeling from my dream earlier had shattered. I debated staying in my room until six, but decided to walk downstairs anyway, as the boys were watching what I would do. I didn't want to give them any satisfaction. As I walked down the stairs, Nicholas pushed past me, catching my shoulder as he went and nudged me into the banister. I didn't know why, but I got the feeling that this boy really didn't like me. Jenny had also appeared at the top of the stairs, bumping me as she walked by, but this time I tripped up and staggered down a few steps. I watched them walk into a room I hadn't noticed earlier and had just started to follow them, when a voice said, "Stay there." I automatically froze on the spot, unsure of why I obeyed the voice. Was I going crazy, or was that a real voice I had just heard? Who heard voices inside their heads and actually listened to them. Oh yeah, that's right. People who are batshit crazy, that's who...

I was so busy questioning my sanity that I didn't see Mr Stevenson glaring at me. I apologised and quickly started to follow him into the room, but as I tried to move, I realised that my ankle was hurting, as if I had twisted it or something. I decided not to say anything about it since Mr Stevenson was already waiting on me, and followed him into the room for dinner.

Thank You

First off, I have no idea how to write a thank you, so if I miss anyone, please forgive me. This is all new to me. To Sue, thank you so much for your honesty and for helping kick my ass. I appreciate every change and I think it's a better story now than it ever was. Thank you for how quickly you managed it and I can't wait to work with you more on the rest of these stories.

I want to thank my fabulous friend Laura. Your mad skills are amazing and this book wouldn't be anywhere near as good as it is without you helping me. Thank you for being one of my best friends. I trust your opinions and I am so grateful for our friendship.

To my wonderful friends thank you all for keeping me sane over these past few years and listening to me when I have been moaning. It is incredible to have such a wonderful group of loyal friends and I count my blessings each and every day that I have all of you in my life. So Tracey, Allie, Aimee, Donna, Lynne, Lindsay and Steff thank you to you all.

Next up, I'd like to thank my amazing writing girls, Katie, Danni, and Charlie. You have all been amazing and I appreciate every push or shove in some cases that you have given me. Katie and Danni, thank you for so many years of friendship. I value you both more than I can express on paper (who knew I was such a sap.) Charlie, thank you so much for the amazing cover for *Candlelight* and for kicking my ass when required. Katie, thank you for the loan of the Burnt Ashes boys. I was so happy you said yes and I am so grateful to have that little nod in there.

I'd also like to thank my family for all of their support, encouragement, and for watching the boys so I could work on this. Mum, Dad, Jen, Gary, Shaz, and Morgan, thank you all so much. To wee Boab, who has sat with me watching TV while I worked, you're an awesome wee guy and an inspiration and to my Gran, I love you very much. To the rest of my mad squad of a family, especially Suz, thanks for all your support; it means the world to me.

To all the people who read this book before it was edited, thank you so, so much, especially those in my street time. You guys rock. Your feedback was incredible and has helped shape the edits and additions to the story. To all the people buying it, thank you so much and I hope you enjoy the stories I have to tell.

I want to finish off by thanking my amazing husband for looking after me and the boys. You are incredible, and I don't tell you nearly enough how much the boys and I love you and appreciate everything you do. Love ya, Spikey. To my babies, everything I do is for you and I love you as far as I can reach. The best surprises I have ever had in life was being gifted both of you.

All my love

Peace out.

Made in the USA
Charleston, SC
18 September 2016